The Voyage
of the
Cauldron Skipper

Thomas Paul Murphy

DEDICATION

To those whose stories are never told.

About the cover: Created by the author, the image of the Mississippi River was photographed by the author from a Monastery located on a bluff high above the river.

CONTENTS

ACKNOWLEDGMENTS

A special thanks to those who helped me with this book; each in their own way. Pat Lafferty moderator of the Milwaukee Writers Workshop Novel Group, Robert Riley, Mary Jean Smoeller Phd. and her creative writing classes at UW Milwaukee, Christie Craig, Amy Rosa, Mary Jean Clark, James Boone Dryden and his Milwaukee Writers Workshop, Filamena Lee and the members of her Writing for Publication Class offered by the Whitefish Bay recreation department, Richard Bennett, Leslie McCormick, Rosalie Roberston, Janet Schwartz, Ambrose Thomas Murphy and JoAnn Murphy.

Thomas Paul Murphy

1 RACE DAY

RB awoke before sunrise and walked outside his riverside home to breathe the fresh morning air. As he looked past the shoreline he saw that the water of the Cauldron River was slowly flowing. The calm surface would soon be rippled by glaring reflections of daylight and the activities to come.

The Cauldron River was one of the larger interconnected rivers on the planet that the earliest dwellers called Path of Water. As the society advanced the more modern and proper name changed to Aqua Caverness, which was meant to more accurately describe the lack of large water basins such as oceans and the prevalence of the more tributary nature of the world.

RB thought of how he had walked to the highest bluffs at this time of day and made a mental map of some of the nearer sections of the misting river that revealed themselves as the river carved its way through rock formations and towering forests.

He looked upstream, in the direction of where the four sisters who comprised the Mayhem family lived, and thought of the youngest, Tamarack. Three days ago he seemed to notice something different about her. He watched her work while he foraged for Mucklums on the river bottom with his long handled scoop net that day. She seemed to look older to him then, as she carried two buckets of Horloff milk to the Horloff churn. The Horloff's were large furry four legged grazing animals with sleepy looking faces. Their coat of fur had thick fibers on back that transitioned into a silky smooth white fur as it extended down to their large distended bellies. Their fur had the ability to partially reflect their surroundings and thereby blend them to their natural habitat.

For some reason this memory of Tamarack replayed in his mind and he could see that her stride was different somehow. Her arms swung gracefully as she walked and to him it signified a sense of drive and purpose, something he had never seen in her older sisters.

She didn't seem to notice him at all, offshore in his boat, so he continued to look that on that day. When she walked back to get another bucket of milk to process with the Horloff churn she took out a list from her shorts pocket. To RB she seemed to read items on the list in a persnickety manner, as if she was being more careful to pay attention to what she was doing. She seemed more determined to him than before. She took care to neatly fold her list and put it in her pocket and he noticed the nuance. It seemed indicate to him that she had developed more of a purpose. He sensed a similar aspect of ambition as he watched her carry that last bucket load of Horloff milk back to the Horloff churn with a stride that was graceful and yet looked to have an unstoppable strength of momentum. He could see how she was proud of herself and not pretentious by the way she dutifully took to her task.

Discreetly he watched from his boat as she mounted the Horloff churn. The Horloff churn was a pedal powered machine her and her sisters used to churn butter from Horloff milk. And the pedals of the machine were indeed made from the hoofs of Horloffs. As she started to pedal the churn RB saw that the smooth and lean muscles of her legs now sharply defined themselves.

He experienced these shades of thought as he sat in his boat that day. Bewildered, he realized this was something he hadn't noticed before. And found himself caught staring as she turned and noticed him. At this distance her eyes seemed glazed over, as she looked his way. Her head was slightly pointed downward and her mouth was sagging a little as she looked at him. RB had seen a similar look to this before and it made him a little nervous as he could not place exactly what it meant, so discreetly he continued about his business of foraging the river bottom with his scoop net.

As he looked down he saw his reflection in the water and noticed that his hair was still mostly dark colored. He liked to think that he looked like a good man who was strong. He never considered himself good looking or ugly, just himself. He couldn't say what women thought of him. From something that he sensed that he could not describe, he believed that he made some uptight.

It occurred to him that he always thought of himself as the same height as everyone he talked to, but the reality was he was usually a lot taller than most. In terms of physical strength he didn't have the widest body as some shorter men did, but his muscles were solid and he was capable of holding his own just as well as others.

RB looked down into the water he saw the choicest scoop of Mucklum. Mucklums were about the size of his hand and had a hard shell, and when they were pried open and eaten they had a hearty natural flavor. The taste often reminded RB of the flavor of a good drink he once tried; a flavor that was said to come from far away. It was a puzzle to many how the Mucklums contrasted in color to the silt which they were scooped from. The vibrantly colored yellow one he saw in the water below the boat was a scarce one indeed.

RB continued to think of Tamarack and remembered that two days ago he had noticed that she was wearing a stylish new tightly smooth woven top the same color of that rare yellow Mucklum. He would have noticed it if he had seen her wear it before because it stood out so much; so he surmised it must have been something she had gotten new or made herself.

It was just yesterday when he went to buy a little Horloff milk, cheese and butter from the four Mayhem sisters place. As he had walked passed Tamarack, who was talking to her older sister Shurlene, Tamarack stuck out her pointed finger in his direction and nearly missed his eye with it.

"You almost took out my eye!" he did indeed say to her. She ignored him and he thought, *"She must have seen me coming by? Did she intentionally try to poke me, as she was spewing vetted words to Shurlene?"* The kvetching words he heard her say to Shurlene reverted back to him, the discourse of them made him a little uncomfortable and uneasy. He felt compelled to remember them; in order to know what the meaning was that he was supposed to know and couldn't figure out.

Tamarack had said this, "I'm not going to put up with this coming, ashores."

And then Shurlene this, "Ashores it is and a ashores it will be's, spoiled milks worth is."

Tamarack, "Indeed a day's worth googling, who needs a day's worth googling milkings."

Shurlene, "Milk of sale, means empties pail, so go churn what's teet and hail."

Tamarack further flushed, "Fillingsworth for Mr. Millingsworth, is why I pedal?"

Hearing this took him a little away from himself and Milkmaid Shurlene seemed a little uptight to him also, when he purchased the Horloff products from them. He reflected, *"This wasn't part of the less formal diction people used amongst themselves, so why were they talking that way? Were they reverting backwards in speech because of a mood?"*

RB realized he could only think too much of these things and to no avail as he took a deep breath of fresh air and walked back inside his home.

'***

RB looked out his kitchen window while he cooked his morning meal. The Path of Water was a fertile planet and provided ample means for making food and shelter. He saw the morning sun brighten the grass by the shoreline as he added a dash of tangleweed into one pot where he had placed a few Mucklums and fresh water. He had caught these himself by scooping them off of the river bottom. They had a hard and crusty hinged shell. In a second pot were some grains that he had handpicked from clearings in the forest. As he stirred the pot of cereal grain he heard his two Moreloaf companions awaken.

Mssr. Von Helmoot was slightly literate. He had a shaggy coat of white fur that was accentuated by spots that were the color of sandy stone river banks. He was just starting to rise along with Pepper Marley Mayhem, a different breed- the younger and smaller of the two. Pepper had short white bristle fur that had a few blotchy spots the color of tossed silt. Though

Pepper was smaller he had tight snappy muscles and a boxy pointed snout.

His quadruped knee-high sidekicks stretched up from their prone positions and shook off the claim the night's rest had on them as they smelled their morning meal was about ready. They appeared quietly at his side, as if savoring the taste already in their mouths. RB then portioned some of his meal into bowls on the floor for the two furbearers.

He imagined the weekly race- to be held this morning between the active members of the Up Falls section of the Cauldron River. It proved not only a source of joyful entertainment, but a competition that formed a sense of community in this sparsely populated region. A display on the wall showed a countdown to the start time. The contestants, all five of them, were to start from their own docks and race toward a buoy that was more or less equal distance between them. Whereupon the course then headed downstream to a second buoy, looped around it and back up to the first one, which was now the finishing point.

RB's vision of the day to come was interrupted by Pepper Marley.

"The gravy more tangy," Pepper said between slurping chops.

Mssr. Von Helmoot, the larger and older of the two, replied, "Make this way more often!"

"Last time I did, one of you complained and said there was some spice you couldn't identify. And I told you then, I only make what's good for you."

"Preposterous!" Pepper slurred.

"Ludicrous!" MSSR Von Helmoot chimed in aloofly.

"Is there anymore left? I would like a second helping," Pepper so stated.

"I always make enough for leftovers. But it's getting to be race time, and we have to head for the Cauldron Skipper," RB said.

"Why do we call the racing boats Cauldron Skippers anyway?" Pepper asked.

"They got their name because when they are going real fast they skip on the surface of the water like skipping stones, and of course because the river here is named the Cauldron River. So therefore we call all of our boats that we use for racing Cauldron Skippers," RB answered as he heard the distant rumble of the other boats starting up.

As for RB's talking Moreloafs, that is a different story. RB would always speak to them as if they were people. Sometimes he would yell if they did something wrong like knock something over. He loved them so much he would even read aloud to them. He could tell they had some sense of understanding. There was more to them than most people would want to admit. One day he had had it with them tracking mud in the place and yelled. "You ever bring mud in again and you will sleep outside for good. I mean- for good!"

Mssr. Von Helmoot miraculously replied, "Not mud, Horloff droop."

Pepper spoke to, "That's right, Horloff droop."

And that is how they learned to talk.

2 THE REINS OF SPHERE

RB's hands were doing the work of cleaning the dishes from their morning meal in his kitchen sink as he reflected on a fortuitous day, not long ago, when he was in his Skipper boat and a new energy source rained from the sky. On that day while napping in his Skipper something was bringing him out of his slumber. He carefully opened his eyes and slowly blinked a few times to ease them from their drylock.

Slowly, he then flexed his hands and then forearms to bring himself out of the sluggish rest. He looked at his fishing line and saw nothing different there. Hearing a swooshing sound he then looked upwards. It seemed an eerie presence was approaching from the sky. Indeed streaming down from out of the sky were what looked like a series of small meteorites!

They impacted the water right off the side of his boat with a splash that sprayed water on his face. RB wiped the water from his face with the bottom of his shirt and took a gander at the floating balls. They seemed to have a semi-transparent green energy intensity. *"They are making a whirling noise as they spin and yet they are staying in place."*

With a discerning squint he studied the objects. He tilted his head to change his point of view and decided they were of no harm.

He thought, *"What would they be good for? They seem to possess energy?"*

He grabbed his long handled scoop net and looked left and right, to see who else would know, and then greedily he scooped one up.

A shimmering intensity was present, an ionic power. He laid the net on the floor of his boat, with the one sphere in it and the intensity of the sphere seemed to resonate within him. He reached out and touched it briefly and it did him no harm. *"They are giving me a healthy feeling,"* he realized. So he gently nudged the one in the net onto out the deck of his boat and went back to the gunwale to scoop up the rest. Before he scooped the ones still in the water he decided to count them and as he thought of counting them they came to a dead stop and remained stationary as they floated. There were fifteen left, so in total there were sixteen. An epiphany struck him, *"That is the same amount of ball cylinders in the motors of my boat."*

As he looked on he thought, *"They are about the size of the green melon I accidently trip over at the foot of the path. I could hold one cupped in my hands."* RB's reserve fuel tank reservoir was empty and clean so he gently picked the sphere on the deck of his boat up and placed it in the tank. As he did so, the sphere increased and decreased in size; as if to mock his analysis. He looked at another one and saw how the water surrounding it was not moving. As soon as he thought this the sphere resonated causing a little commotion and some ripples.

As he studied another one, he thought, *"They float very well."* As he thought this, the sphere made a popping sound and dove under the water. It popped back up and tilted left and right twice and then abruptly stopped this motion. He then changed his focus to look at the spheres all together as a group, and thought, *"They all appear to look the same,"* each one then turned into a different color.

"They must all have a base color to revert to sometimes," was followed with each one changing color patterns at random. Some were the prior colors of the others. But no two were ever the same color at the same time. They were of translucent greens, ambers, silvers, oranges, reds, purples, blues, yellows and gold's. All seemed to draw his eyes past their surface and inward; to know the realm of there essence. As he stared his gaze took him into what seemed to be an infinite distance of surrealism.

"They seem to possess a dimension of reality or oneness to ancient life origins," he thought this without knowing why.

His next thought, *"Their choice of colors seems to be distinctly constant,"* was followed by each orb transitioning through the full color spectrum, again independent of one another. He then wondered, *"Are they always at odds with one another?"* All of them then turned translucent green again and were uniform to one another.

One by one he scooped them up and laid them onto the floor of his boat. When he went to scoop up the last one, it scuttled about with a screeching laughter. Playfully spinning to get away, but not trying too hard- it dodged two of RB's attempts to scoop it. RB saw the way it moved and that if it had wanted to get away, it would have been easy for it to do so.

On a whim he unlatched the chamber lids that held the original spinning orb drives for his motors and set one of the new energy spheres on top of the orb in the spherical combustion chamber. His combustion chambers could be turned on and off as power was needed and this one had been turned off. The energy sphere displaced itself to the ball shaped orb drive and became one with it. Fuel looked to be displaced from the orb combustion chamber back into the primary fuel tank.

"They won't let fuel from my tank enter the motor," he realized as fuel was indeed being displaced from entering the cylinders by the presence of the spheres in the tank as the motor ran. It looked to be a surreptitious discovery of invention so he left it that way.

"These spheres fell out of the sky!" he thought in wonderment. The boat had started moving forward after the motors turned themselves on, so he decided to see how it now operated. For the same amount of throttle his speed seemed to have increased tremendously from what the engine was capable of attaining before, and there were no longer any fumes from his motors exhaust ports, his engines seemed quieter and therefore efficient. *"They now have the capability of turning the driveshaft at a higher maximum level of comparative revolutions per moment!"*

"Visual status reservoir fuel tank," RB commanded ships control system module as he steered the boat. He looked at his boats control system and specifically to the fuel system monitor.

"That's not right!"- The reservoir was empty of the orbs. *"What is that in the lower corner of my fuel reservoir where the fuel transfers into the motor from? ...One of the spheres is transforming its shape into a linear form and squeezing itself into my motors main fuel supply line!"*

"The rest must have done the same," he surmised as he recognized his pattern of thinking to be, *"I put two and two together to form a deductive conclusion regarding the now empty reservoir."* The boat sped up further. He looked at his throttle; somehow

he was at one quarter throttle, but yet going as fast as he had before, when he was at full throttle.

"If I manually go to full throttle, will I be in danger of capsizing?" Upon thinking this the boat banked sharply left on its own and then right and then straightened to a dead arrow course with the river channel.

"I could have been thrown from the boat!" The boat then banked left and right as a new pattern of gravity held his feet firm onto the deck.

"The way my feet held firm to the deck there was no way I could have fallen out." His right foot then became free of the localized gravity force and a sense of fear welled up in him quickly. But the concern diminished just as quickly as the invisible grasp took a gravity hold of his foot again. *"With this much power I could navigate the whole planet!"*

'***

This memory of that day faded as the dishes were finished, and he thought, *"The reward for a job well done is to take pride in a job well done. This leads to others recognizing a job well done. How long should one bask in pride before it is best to start thinking forward of the next accomplishment? A distraction from pride would seem to lead one forward?"*

3 THE RACE

RB had done a lot of work on his sleek boat and it looked like he and his two crewmates might have an edge in the river boat race against Tamarack Mayhem and her three older sisters; Cherry Bo Berry, Milkmaid Shurlene and Medika Mayhem. He had not won in quite some time and mused, *"Maybe this time will be different, with the help of my new spheres, I am going to win today! And if I do the sisters will probably jest and say that I cheated."*

He walked to the dock, untied the cleated knot that his father had taught him, the one that safely bastioned the boat, and hopped in his Cauldron Skipper. He fired up all sixteen combustion ball chambers of the twin engines. The engines were held firm within the double wall reinforced hull of his Cauldron Skipper. The initial percussion of the contained energy conversion release of the motors gave him a renewed sense of vigor. They sputtered momentarily before quickly coming to a hum; a sound that RB had come to rely on in confidence time after time. This early sense of vitality would carry him through the day. The power of these motors was quite formidable. The boat was the color of the translucent red

Mucklums that he found in choice places on the bottom of the Cauldron River. His boats profile was close to the surface and he had dynamically designed to navigate swiftly through the most treacherous of waters. Integral to hull design was a compensating ballast that lessened the threat of the boat capsizing.

His four legged companions Mssr. Von Helmoot and Pepper Marley Mayhem scampered and skipped to the pier to join him and hopped in their bow mounted observation pods. They pulled their respective levers and semicircle windshields rolled up into place. They heard RB Rough's voice boom their final procedural commands, "Engage forward system protocol."

Mssr. Von Helmoot and Pepper Marley Mayhem each turned their respective knobs by pawing at them and windshield wipers appeared from below and engaged. It wasn't going to rain but there would be plenty of water kicked up. RB then levered the gradient drive shaft transmission and the boat was underway.

As they glided forward toward the buoy ahead of them in the race he turned briefly to look back at the scenery and could see the dark clouds of evil black smoke rising in the aft-ward distance. Tamarack Mayhem, the youngest of the four highly competitive sisters, was powering toward him in her Cauldron Skipper. Her scuffed black colored boat was diabolically designed. It had a latticework platform that narrowed at the perch where she sat judging the water currents. She was obsessed with winning the race. Her boat had no safety screen, unlike RB's.

'***

The origins of the race date back to the most primitive forms of boats, dugouts or bundled reeds that were pushed with poles. With a sense of camaraderie they had raced to get to the best fishing spots first. As technology advanced on the planet, the boats became stronger and more advanced drive systems were developed. Once somebody did something good the others got jealous and tried in the worst way to outdo one another. And that is how technology advanced on the planet. It was a backwards forwards manner based upon competition; as was the boat race. Up Falls members would stay up all night chewing their teeth trying to outthink or out invent the one with the best ideas. Often just out of frustration someone would try something whimsical or tinker with something and serendipitously invent something new. Through this process, the boats became stronger and faster and the race more competitive.

'***

The current boat hull compositions were based on the legend of Sirus Mayhem. One day Sirus Mayhem, an ancestor of the four racing sisters, had noticed that his Horloffs had eaten a dark sappy reed plant. He could see some of it on the corners of their jowls. They seemed to like it as their eyes got droopy and one was seen rolling on the ground. The milk they produced was darker in color and more viscous from grazing on the sappy plant. He tried a taste of it and spat it out right away as if it were poison. And the whole batch of milk had to be dumped.

Sirus took the foul milk a little walks distance from his home and poured it into a depressed round basin in the ground. It just sat there and didn't sink all the way down into the soil, so

Sirus started to worry, *"What if someone came walking along and accidently fell into this, they might drown in this goop!"* So Sirus then found some strong natural fibrous plants and placed them over the sap to cover it. It still kind of looked dangerous so he found some silver colored metal powder, they now call Tucci, and threw it over the goop. Because it still bothered him, he decided some hot sands might thicken it further. He found some dry sands in a sunny spot and very quickly sifted them over everything else he had thrown in. Much to his surprise the hot mineral sands turned a translucent green. The material at this stage is now known to be called Gritallia. The Gritallia then further catalyzed the solution base containing the Horloff milk. The silver metal Tucci ran into the fibrous vein like formations and in combination with them formed what looked like what might have a latticework of strength. Sirus was relieved as the sap that initially posed such a great danger to the safety others, hardened. The structure or dome created was thin and yet rock solid.

After a few days of marveling at it, Sirus grabbed a pole, pried the dome shaped form out of its basin and dragged it to the water. He nudged it in the water and it floated. Fearful that it might partially or fully dissolve he sat on the shore and held it with his pole to keep it near. After a little while he tried to push it down into the water with the side of his pole. Because of the way it wobbled back from the push he knew it had some stability. He sat on shore with it floating next to him in the water. In very little time he became bored of holding it with the pole. He did not feel like dragging it out of the water. Out of curiosity he wanted to know if it would hold him or sink. As he tried carefully to get in the saucer he slipped. He let go of his pole as he then landed awkwardly and feel on his bottom in the saucer. The saucer rocked back and forth. He grabbed his pole before it could float away as the saucer stabilized. Sirus looked and saw that he was not sinking. He started to float about in the saucer. Pushing with his pole the boat moved faster and responded quicker than any other he had been in.

As he sat in it he noted the process by which it was created. Over time the formula became more refined and thereby better and the resulting hull forms sleeker, stronger and faster. The composite material became the basis for much of their structural technology.

'***

Tamarack's long dark hair, the consistency of sun dried tangleweed, flew about chaotically ahead of the evil plumes that toxically trailed her boat. Protruding dauntingly out of the right corner of her mouth was an elongated black cob pipe that fumed almost as bad as her boat. She sat atop her speeding boat with a hunched back and a lurching forward crooked neck. Helmoots ears cringed upon hearing the ill timed motors.

The buoy they were approaching gave the start signal by flashing a red light beam out to its sides in a horizontal plane above the water's surface.

RB saw the start signal, but as he felt her approaching from behind, he realized his engines were not at full operating temperature. His heart sank as he saw the curved series of blackened tail foils pass him by, with her sense of arrogance-off the trailing end of her Cauldron Skipper.

He briefly caught sight of her evil smirk as she overtook him. But what really got his sea warrior spirit aroused was that life choking black mist that trailed and fumed out the widely diametered tangled exhaust ports of her Cauldron Skipper.

This was more than he could stand and he engaged the solar captive panel switch on his Skipper boat. The solar cell plating on the bow of his skipper turned a heated crimson red. This raised his boats operating temperature to core efficiency and provided additional thrust conversion for the motors.

"I am back in the race!"

Mssr. Von Helmoot and Pepper Marley Mayhem, his faithful crew, alternately bobbed their heads at the stern of the Cauldron Skipper they were approaching. RB then rapidly overtook Tamarack Mayhem on the outside of the turn buoy with his motors at full operating temperature.

In a panicked fit, Tamarack turned too quickly and her Cauldron Skipper did a half moon turn and the motor stalled. Tamarack's boat was dead in the water. She stood up on her platform and with a scolding wretched tone yelled, "It's not over yet!"

Upon seeing Tamarack out of the race RB relaxed and powered down his twin propulsion drives to a more efficient speed as he made his way back to the starting point; assured of his victory. But his moment of complacency rapidly diminished when he heard the loud moan of what looked to be a second Cauldron Skipper from another racer rapidly approaching from behind.

This black boat was somewhat identical to Tamarack's except the markings on the side of the hull read "C Bo Berry" and the name was preceded by a painted on bunch of red berries. Assured of power he allowed the second black Cauldron Skipper to get alongside his boat so he might identify his competitor.

RB looked at the operator of the boat to his side and indeed saw that it was Cherry Bo Berry, the nicest of Tamarack's three sisters. Cherry Bo Berry had a similar getup to that of Tamarack, but she wore a vibrant red polymer racing suit, the shine of which glistened through the haze. Cherry spryed at him with a menacing gloat.

With her vibrantly red colored scarf flailing behind her in the racing wind she howled out at him, "You're finished!" and pulled her throttle to full bore. She then overtook him.

RB Rough thought to himself, *"I've got more to my boat than that,"* and then in turn to her remark pulled back the throttle to full bore. The twin motors now hummed like never before and the corresponding drive propellers whirled out proud arcing tails of water. They rained confidently behind his streamlined Cauldron Skipper.

The two boats were now neck and neck as they each could see the finish line in the distance. It was then that C- Bo Berry stood up and put all the weight of her right foot on the platform floor mounted power assist accelerator. Her boat started to slowly nudge past and overtake RB's.

"Where is the extra power from my energy spheres?" RB silently asked himself. The boat then sped ahead past C-Bo Berry's.

Cherry then reached for the lever that both opened and controlled the air intake to her engine. She added a liquid derivative of sappy reed plant to her fuel supply. Her boat then sped ahead of RB's. RB heard screeching laughter coming from his energy spheres that had rained to him from the sky and then his boat then lost speed. At which point Cherry Bo Berry increased her lead on RB in the race.

Mssr. Von Helmoot and Pepper Marley Mayhem were not keen on losing and barked back at RB, "Don't worry. We're with you!"

Helmoot and Pepper, for short, turned to each other in serious unison and gave each other the: *"We know what we have to do,"* look. They quickly activated their respective manual power assist levers and the doors to the lower operating unit beneath them opened and all eight of their paw boat shoes locked into the pedal power assist mechanism. The super high ratio transmission drives of the pedal powered assist mechanisms then advanced seamlessly onto the forward ends of the main drive shafts of RB's Cauldron Skipper via a system that coordinated drive shaft speed upon union.

Once drive shaft union was achieved a jolt of speed was felt as the Moreloafs put forth exhaustive efforts and full power transmission of their efforts commenced.

Each Moreloaf pedaled all four paws in frantic rapid unison with the other and summoned the residing spirit of Moreloafs from history that pulled sleds on trails. In little time their red Skipper nudged past the C-Bo Berry's Cauldron Skipper at the finish line to win the day's race.

RB slowed his boat as Cherry Bo Berry Mayhem caught up alongside of him. In light hearted humor he gave a respectful salute to Cherry Bo Berry as Helmoot and Pepper, already disengaged from their bio energy assist efforts, hopped about gleefully on the flat part of the deck.

RB saw C-Bo Berry's red scarf still flowing in the breeze and this cued him in on danger. Rather abruptly, and to the astonishment of Helmoot and Pepper, he commanded them, "Resume operating positions!" They dutifully hopped to their pedals before he was able to announce the materiality of his concern to them; "Our competitor is in a dire situation!"

RB Rough knew he had unfinished business and that his reckless former competitor, in this days race, was still stranded and now in possible peril. He engaged full throttle and commenced a one hundred and eighty degree turn. His Cauldron Skipper turned outwardly and away from C Bo Berry's so fast that if it had been attempted with most other ordinary boats they likely would have capsized. He then sped back to search for Tamarack and her Cauldron Skipper.

The boat cruised at near top speed for awhile before he could see from a great distance that Tamarack's anchor wasn't holding and without her fume drive, she was rapidly drifting towards the falls with their rock laden eminent danger awaiting below. Mssr. Von Helmoot and Pepper Marley Mayhem knew of the terminate danger and looked back at RB in horror as their master did not cut his speed.

RB activated his Sonic Audio Boom that magnified his voice and commanded to Mssr. Von Helmoot and Pepper Marley Mayhem, "ENGAGE FULL SAFETY PROTOCOLS." In spite of their fear they managed to follow the command immediately.

He glanced at the stalled Cauldron Skipper with its smoking engines on his way to the falls and then pounded on the rightward of his three full momentum stop brakes. His boat stopped all forward progress. He instantly turned his boat, placing it between his reckless competitor and the falls. He put his life in harm's way for Tamarack.

RB's voice boomed loudly once again as the defunct Cauldron Skipper, caught in the current, approached along his portside, "Jump aboard before it is too late and all is lost!" As the scene from his vision became clearer in those quick moments he could see that Tamarack was sobbing; in a fearful shaking quiver.

Marley Mayhem looked at Von Helmoot again, *"that way,"* for the last time that day, as if to say, *"Here we go again,"* and they rapidly resumed their pedal assisted routine. But this time two small round doors on the starboard side opened. Two worm drive propellers were already spinning as they extended from the portals into the water. Located in a balanced position fore and aft they provided lateral support that fought against the current.

The deafening sound of the waterfall was then heard by the four of them. There was a sensation of electricity felt as the ions of oxygen were stripped from the water molecules and they started to feel the percussive roar from the liquids drop.

The cascading water was a natural leveling process that cleansed as it balanced life.

Dimly, Tamarack looked one last time to and fro or her long proud Cauldron Skipper and leapt onto RB's sleek red Skipper. RB caught her safely and embraced her as she landed in his boat. He held her briefly then in his arms and for just a moment their eye's met and each recognized the passion they saw in the other.

RB then let go of her as she sat down in defeat and watched her boat edge its way to the falls. Quickly he then swung his boat in a half circle around Tamarack's and they were out of the perilous predicament of being close to the edge. With Tamarack safely in his boat he was now a short distance further upstream in the rivers current than her perilously Cauldron Skipper. And upon seeing the distraught look on Tamarack's face as she looked at her boat that was about to succumb to a rocky end, out of the kindness of his heart, he pulled a lever and a tractor line shot out of a port hole that opened on the aft of his boat. The fixture on the end of the line stuck promptly to the hull of Tamarack's still smoking Cauldron Skipper. Swiftly her boat had drifted still closer to the edge. *"Clunk,"* it bumped a rock in current and then, *"clunk"* it bumped another one. The water was more shallow and fast near where it dropped off at the waterfall. Her abandoned Skipper picked up speed in the rapidly moving water, and *"Clunk, Clunk,"* it bumped another two rocks. The sound of the *"Clunks"* felt like a cold blow to her lungs. The boat bumped its way on more rocks and started to angle over the falls!

Tamarack's heart sank as she watched it happen. RB's boat was still holding strong to hers via the tow line but as the speed of the current increased the closer they got to the edge- they were going with it! He quickly set the spool of his winch so that line could freely flow out, but he only had so much line and so little time. Her boat was now angling further downward- about to fall out of sight- over the falls. If he didn't act quickly they would be on the way down too as they were towing fast to hers.

The tow line was woven from a fiber synthesized from Horloff milk and formed in such a way so that it could never be broken by known forces. With a sad look on his face he knew what he had to do, "If I don't all will be lost!" He thought frantically and jettisoned the spiral winch the tow line was coiled to.

Still holding fast to her boat the spiral winch sprang toward her boat with a snapping sound and her Cauldron Skipper swiftly tilted all the way over the rocks at the ledge and sunk from their view.

Rather somberly RB snapped up a safety panel exposing a lever he had never had to use before. Unknown to Tamarack he flipped a different switch. He then immediately heard the telltale poof sound as the spool winch control module safety protocol immediately self destructed and blew itself up along with her ill-fated Cauldron Skipper. The sound of the explosion was lost to her ears in the haze of the misting waterfall as RB pulled them out raging current and into safety.

As RB's shimmering red metallic Skipper vectored towards home ports, Tamarack looked up at him with sad eyes and said, "My reckless strive for victory and disregard for safety almost cost me my life. I don't know how I can ever reward you for your valiant rescue."

Seeing that Tamarack was shivering, RB pulled her close to him and said softly, "It would not have been me to do otherwise, and the race would not be the same without you." He then draped a soft blanket around her shoulders. They gazed into each other's eyes and shared another warm embrace. RB felt her body next to his and he was momentarily pleased.

As his Skipper rode merrily across the surface of the water, Tamarack, seated equidistance between RB and his crew, pulled out a wretched looking black fish bone comb from her front shirt pocket and turned her head slightly to the right as she combed that side while not looking back at RB.

4 THE JAUNT HOME

RB had three boat mates now. They race was over and they were taking Tamarack home. They had just passed his dock by a few boat lengths on their way to Tamarack's when RB looked at her. She had long finished combing her windblown mess of unkempt hair into a straight glossy jet black sheen that captivated and absorbed all but the most resilient rays of the sun, or a man's gaze when Tamarack slowly turned in her seat to RB but did not look up at him.

RB thought, *"She swung the whole of the beautiful lock over her left shoulder,"* and for once in his life, RB could look at nothing else but this display. He found himself staring at the glistening mass as if the gravity of his mind could not escape it. An energy was welling up inside him like he had never known in his life. He tried to speak but was unable to as he realized, *"I am drawn to her like her boat was to the Cauldron Falls!"*

Tamarack gazed up at him with longing eyes and provided an easement by breaking the silence first, "My ported bungalow could only be accessed via my Cauldron Skipper, solely and exclusively," her words sauntered on, "There currently is no way for me to accommodate myself there anymore."

Somehow RB's spirit was revitalized by a new sense of chivalry. He said gallantly, "It is a hero's honor to help a maiden in distress. I will provide you with all the accommodations you need while you recover from the loss of your Cauldron Skipper."

"I will accept your hospitality," Tamarack replied.

"Me and the lads have a picnic lunch. There is a sunny alcove with a sandy beach just around the bend here. I have enough for you also," RB said.

"That sounds wonderful," Tamarack responded.

RB was convinced that that meant she wanted to eat there too and that it was a noble thing to do to treat her to lunch. He maneuvered his boat slowly to turn to approach the shore. A peaceful wake of water followed. RB's boat slowly ran aground of the sandy shore. He got out at the front of the boat and beached it to shore by pulling it further up onto the land. He reached back in the bow and lifted the heavy anchor up and set it safely down on the dry shore a few steps inland.

"Do you know how to tie a quick release knot?" RB asked.

"Maybe not the one you're tying," she said while peering over his shoulder at what he was doing. RB could feel the warmness of her aura as she looked intently at what he was doing. As he took up the slack and tied the knot, he realized he was teaching her something and that a oneness was felt between them. He saw how innocent she looked as she watched in anticipation of learning how he would finish. RB grabbed the rope on both sides of the knot and pulled, "It will not come apart," handing it to her he said, "Now you try."

She pulled strongly and said, "You're right."

Pointing to a loop in the knot he said, "Now, pull right here."

She did and said, "It falls right apart. That's amazing."

"Many things of this I know," RB said with a wry smile.

"Yes you do," Tamarack countered.

RB reached for Tamarack's hand for her to join him on the pleasant shore. She offered her hand into his. As she extended one leg to shore he felt the closeness of her to him. His eyes were again drawn to her gracefully strong legs. He saw how they defined themselves as her foot dipped into the sand and she cantilevered her other leg out from the boat to land stoutly on shore.

"How do you stay in such great form?" RB asked.

"The youngest of four sisters, it's a necessity," she stated with a nonchalant smile.

"I'll grab the blanket and lunch," he said as he opened a storage compartment in his boat.

He grabbed a tarpaulin made of woven Horloff hide and a duffle with food in it and closed the lid.

Laying out the blanket he said, "I have some mineral cured fish, crackers and a hearty Horloff milk drink of my own concoction, I think you might like."

"And just how did you make this concoction?"

"I added two sprigs of Red Berries leaf, and three worth of powdered stink mint leaf. Plus some sweet sap from a White Syrup Bark tree found back a ways in the forest."

He poured some for each and she took a sip.

"It's very good," she said, sounding surprised.

"Thank you," he replied.

"My older sisters don't experiment too much with cooking like you seem to."

"On my own, I learned to cook through experiment," RB said.

They sat and lunched some on mineral cured fish and crackers and the hearty Horloff milk drink of his concoction.

RB was done eating first and said, "I usually read a new story aloud at this time to Mssr. Von Helmoot and Pepper. Would you like to hear one also?"

"Sure," Tamarack replied.

RB cleared his throat with a groan that sounded like that of a growling beast hidden in the woods and started to read.

"This one is called, The Poisoned Land Pair Able and it is written by Wembly Willows."

"You mean 'Parable' not 'Pair Able'," Tamarack corrected.

"No it say's 'Pair Able'," RB replied.

"Why is it called that?" Pepper interrupted.

"I don't know, we'll have to read it first to find out," RB said tersely and continued to read.

There was a path that formed into two paths. One led to Mr. Judley's house. Judley had a wife and four children and was regarded as the smartest man in the community. On the other path was Judley's nearest neighbor, Mr. Stan. A hard laboring man, Stan also had a wife but only two children.

One day Judley was walking down the common path when he saw Stan working about.

"What's got you digging today Stan?" Judley asked.

"I received this shiny red metal a man gave him as a gift for helping him build a house and am burying it here…," Stan replied.

Judley saw the ruby colored metal but did not let Stan know of the Crimsmetal's true worth.

Judley paused while he leered at the Crimsmetal until he said, "Looks like a good place for it," and continued on his way.

Stan trusted what Judley told him.

When Judley got home, he thought of the fancy silk and jewels he could give his wife and how their status could be further elevated. He then told his family, "I am going to do something very good for you soon."

The next day Judley's family attended a social function in the more urban part of the community and stayed at his wife's sister's house. Knowing his family would be gone the next two nights, Judley went out during the night and dug a hole on the path to his neighbor's house and loosely covered it up with brush. Along side of it he piled some rocks. After this it started to rain. When he went out the next morning he saw that his trap has sprung and the hole had filled itself in, burying his neighbor under rocks and dirt.

Greedily he grabbed his shovel and ran to dig up his neighbor's buried Crimsmetal. He dug deeper and deeper until he finally saw the reflection of the dense metal. Just then the town constable came walking along and saw him doing this. The constable said, "Lending a hand to Stan today are you?"

"Yes … I am helping Stan dig a well while he went on an errand."

"How are your wife and family doing Judley?" the constable asked.

"They are at my sister-in-law's house all weekend for a community social."

"They aren't in town anymore. They left last night. They told us that you had something really good planned for them and they felt guilty being there in town rather than at home with you."

As the two were talking Stan came walking on the path from his house.

"Hello!" Stan said as he greeted the two with a smile. He continued speaking, "Always nice of you Judley to lend a hand. You don't have to go to all this trouble, I am sure you have better things to do at home with your family."

Judley started to pale as he saw Stan and replied, "I think I will go ahead and do that then."

He headed home with his shovel and found that his family was not at his house and then he wondered, "If they are not in town and not at my house, where could they be? Did they take the wrong path home?...Oh my God!" he screamed in horror and grabbed his shovel again. He ran to the trap he built for Stan and started digging. He found his family dead, buried under the rocks and dirt just as he had planned for Stan.

Judley was full of sorrow for awhile and told no one of what happened. If people were to ask where his family is he would say, "They left me."

One day he started thinking again, "This is all Stan's fault that my family is dead. I am the smartest man in the community. Therefore it cannot be my fault! Stan owes me my family, he does, or at least that Crimsmetal. I'm going at night to dig up his Crimsmetal. Stan has no idea what he's worth."

Knowing exactly where the Crimsmetal was buried, that night Judley grabbed his shovel and headed down the path. He put the full weight of his right foot on the shovel and fell head first into the dense metal. Judleys' head swelled up to the size of a knotty green melon and ever after was thought of as the village idiot.

It turns out that Stan had spread the fresh soil, that Judley had dug up, in rows and planted vegetables to feed his family."

***

"I have heard of legends similar to that. Kind of poetic in terms of his fate," Tamarack stated.

Mssr. Von Helmoot chimed in, "What made him do such a thing to Mr. Stan?"

Pepper said, "Maybe he just became possessed by greed or something."

"The Crimsmetal sure had a draw on him. The parable implied he did it to make his wife happy," RB answered.

"She didn't need all that," Tamarack chimed in.

And with that the discussion of the parable ended.

5 TROUBLE?

They sat in the sun for awhile before RB decided it was time to get back in the boat.

"Do you ever think that Aqua Caverness might not have had as much water as it did at one point in its history or at a prior point in its history that it had a lot more water?"

"I do think of that sometimes but it is hard to think differently than what is because I am accustomed to what is, as if it has always been what is. Kind of like it is not for me to think of how things should be different. It might be curse like to think things should be different."

'***

"Did you just mumble-spur me," RB said to Tamarack.

"Well no I didn't just mumble-spur you," Tamarack replied.

"I thought I heard you just mumble-spur me?" RB said.

"I told you that I did not."

"Are you sure that you did not just say something like, 'I could …with you…right here… on the beach…and no-one would notice?'"

"No!"

As RB packed the picnic items Tamarack said, "Do you mind if I go for a little swim to beat the heat?"

"Not at all."

Tamarack walked out a few steps and quickly removed her clothes and tossed them in the boat. Before RB could see much, she dove just under the surface of the water and started swimming.

Tamarack took elegant and powerful strides. Her legs and arms seemed to move her great lengths with little effort. The form of her body in the water looked very graceful to RB. There was little disturbance as she glided forward and her strokes displaced water. He saw a union of form and purpose between her and the water.

RB felt a little amiss in this forbidden moment, as a harmony was readily created between them, as if they were one from the beginning of time.

In a few fast strides she swam further away from shore and the boat. Then RB watched her feet kick above the surface as she dove under. RB expected her to come back up quickly and it seemed like she had been down under the surface for an eternity. *"Has she found something interesting down there she is trying to bring up or has she been caught on some branches or weeds?"* He wondered while he looked to place she dove under. He then heard the water swish on the opposite side of the boat. When he turned to look he saw Tamarack had broken the water's surface. With a delightful smile she looked at RB and quickly started to swim back to the boat.

"You swim as if you are a fish," RB said as she approached.

"Thank you; I can beat any of my sisters in a race," Tamarack replied as RB reached out his hand to help her in.

They looked in each other's eyes again as he helped her in the boat. And they were soon free of the shore and coasting.

'***

On this last "leg" of the race that was long over Tamarack started to chat profusely. *The speed of her words rivals that of the revolutions attainable by engine number one and motor number two safely contained in the hull of my Skipper."*

"You know how electricity was discovered, don't you RB?"

"Why don't you tell me the story."

"My sisters tell me that one of the earliest Mayhems, Lenora Mayhem, knitted herself a scarf out of milled Ferroweed. She was so proud of the prismatic scarf as it glistened and reflected in the sun that she ran around all day with it streaming behind her. Wound up with so much energy later in the day she got in a boat. Then all of a sudden the wind picked up and a storm was upon her. The wind was taking her boat counter to the current and fast. At the water's edge a crowd had gathered and they were yelling, 'Shore the boat Lenora, shore the boat,' when all of a sudden a loud boom followed a bolt of light that came down from the clouds. The bolt of light touched Lenora's new scarf and it became illuminated as it absorbed the energy. Then her hair stuck straight out from her head like flat spokes. Lenora's hair stayed that way for the rest of her life and one of her daughters was born with that new flat spoke hair also. That's where Cherry is said to get hers from. Any way the community believed that a mystical governing spirit force struck her in this way for her being so vain. Lenora could not stand the implication of this so she set about to disprove it. "No governing spirit force could ever be mad at me," she was heard saying. She started knitting scarf after scarf after scarf.

Then one day a storm came. She went about and raised all the scarves to the tops of trees via some ropes.

By this time another crowd had developed to see just what would happen 'this time' to Lenora. 'Maybe a light bolt will hit her again and turn her hair straight,' one watcher said.

Sure enough, Lenora proved herself right as a bolt of light hit a scarf in a tree. The scarf lit up; just like the one she wore that fateful day.

At the base of the tree she had a ball of yarn attached to the scarf by a long strand that ran down the side of the tree and the ball of yarn glowed for some time. Lenora took a very fine strip of Tunglemetal she had readied and grabbed it with a pair of sticks. She had knitted the balls of yarn so the end of the yarn that would have normally been wound and hidden in the center was sticking out the side. She touched the ends of the Tunglemetal that she held with her sticks to the respective ends of the string of yarn and the small strip of Tunglemetal glowed. She disproved everyone's accusation and discovered electricity!"

"Well, how exactly do you account for Cherry's flat spoked hair?"

"That's just the effect it had on her metabolic being, the electricity fixed it to some form of Lenora that passed on to some later generations, sometimes skipping a few."

"You Mayhems take credit for everything."

"She also invented the yarn ball lantern."

"Remarkable," RB replied.

"Did you ever think of how we developed all this technology, but it all seems to be centered on boats and we don't have much good stuff for anything else?"

"I don't exactly know why we are that way... I have heard legends that our world was once very different, so for some reason we are driven to focus on things that keep us afloat," RB answered.

While she talked RB felt a sense of ease, like none he had ever experienced before in his life. *"My mind is as clear as the blue sky,"* he thought. He extended the steering wheel of his RB Skipper to upright mode and stood proud, straight and tall. All the while hearing her succession of words, he gazed into the ever changing destination points of reference that he used as navigation helpers. Some of these navigation markers were tall trees of permanence that stood above the other's, some were formations of rocks, sandy shore areas and shore areas that were clear of brush or trees. Generally he found things that stood out and were easy to remember made good waypoint landmarks.

RB did not seem in as much of a mood for a fast pace, and slowed his engines to ultra low cruising speed. His Skipper then slowly glided the peaceful waters. The natural surroundings they were experiencing seemed to be in a state of harmony.

It was then that RB tried to analyze what he was experiencing, all he could come up with in his internal dialogue of thought was, *"What type of beautiful magic is this?"* He often thought of feelings in his own terms and wondered if things such as this could be named.

In the far distance RB could just make out the wide mouth of the inlet to his humble and meager stone manor. He was then brought back to the present from the surreal by Tamarack's voice; as something she said seemed to make him think. She had said, "…and of course we'll retrieve my boat afterwards…"

His thoughts of what to say next were interrupted because he heard a muffled rumbling noise and was unsure of its origin or vector. He felt a sudden sense of apoplexy and a quizzical look formed on his face. In order to listen more carefully he put his motors in full silent running mode without changing velocity.

Tamarack was looking downward, her eye's averting him as she was slightly ashamed of what her intuition was telling her; regarding the noise, from- what she knew was approaching.

RB gazed forward and then aft repetitively to determine the origin. He sensed one sound from the direction of the falls but knew that had there been a boat that way, he and his now expanded crew would have noticed it on the jaunt back.

'***

Milk Maid Shurlene was fiercely powering up the throttle of her spotted cow patterned Cauldron Skipper, from a location far below the Cauldron Falls. Her Cauldron Skipper was deceptively disguised as a Milk Maid Boat while being essentially the same as the others- a fast racing boat. It was decorated with white blotchy spots and mounted on the bow was mega sized Horloff cow bell. It sounded off as the boat moved about the waves so as to ease, or unease as it were, the guard of those in her path. A bucket similarly painted as the boat, hung at arms level on a shepherd's hook that was mounted securely to the deck, presumably for transportation and delivery of Horloff milk.

With legs bent at the knees to absorb compromising balance, she wretchedly held onto the steering wheel with a white knuckled grip and put her Cauldron Skipper christened,

"Mooky Booky" into full throttle. She headed with eyes of rage straight up river.

At the appropriate moment she swung the boat rightward and up into the "Secret Oxbow Falls Passage." Her face was pointed to the daytime heavens and with cackling words she yelled, "Fooled Yah!" The boat then took an angled upward ascent course on the choppy water passage that was less steep than the main waterfall. The passage, although somewhat in the traditional shape of an oxbow, had a few turns in it that swung her ever compensating stance about with the motion.

The waters of the oxbow rocked Shurlene's Skipper as she raced through them until she reached a point where her boat shot upward over the apex of the Secret Oxbow Falls and arced forward in flight. Her Mooky Booky was shifted by the wind and its own inherent aerial instability, but landed plumply dead-on up current on the river at a point further upstream from the waterfall.

The Mook Booky Boat was adorned with Horloff Bull horns on the front of the helm. The horns were a chosen addition of hers to the boat for the element of décor they provided. That is what she told everyone regarding the statement they made. But really she liked to think she was a Horloff Bull herself as she raced her boat while peering through the opening of them. The abrupt landing stopped forward momentum and threw Shurlene's upper body over and down into the crux of the Horns.

As the boat landed the cow bell clanged and finished several chaotic revolutions as it swiveled on the shepherd's hook. The boat was almost done leveling itself when Shurlene composed herself and then looked left and right in anger. She then stood up out of her forward leaning position. She thought for a moment and then disengaged the automatic motor brake. With a menacing grin, she then shifted her Mooky Booky Milk Maid Boat directly to full throttle.

At an equal distance up current from RB as Shurlene was down current from him, was Medika Mayhem. She approached him on an intercept course too. The color of Medika Mayhem's boat was redder than the eye's of the devil. On the front were mounted two enormous beady black Mucklum stones that resembled cold hearted eyes. Extending from the very front sides of the bow were two claws that curved inward to form a point at their ends. They were delightfully snapping intermittently while they bobbed ever so slightly with the steadying forward motion of the boat. The boat tore up the glass surface of the water as she approached in rage. On the transom of her boat, that's the rear, were two concave indentations where her propellers protruded from her hull down into the water. Her boat, much like RB's, had two motors but unlike his she named them to her liking. Looking back over her left side, that motor she called "Goose One" looking over her right shoulder that motor she called "Goose Two."

Medika Mayhem carried a long house whip in each hand and upon her discretion would glance backwards and give one of the manually assisted fuel filter cleaning modules a crack with the whip. This provided an added burst of power as contaminants in the filters were flushed to a holding reservoir and the flow of fuel was less restricted. As she cracked the modules with the whip sometimes she yelled, "Give me juicy Goosey," or sometimes if the situation was extreme she would yell in a throaty tone, "Goose juice me!" River folk knew this novelty was an integral part of her competitive racing persona.

She moved into an evil leering composure as she spied RB's Skipper slowly easing itself along the surface, while at the same time she spotted Shurlene's boat rapidly approaching RB on a demolishing drive course.

RB's tranquil mind was now becoming choppy as he realized that two Cauldron Skippers were prowling toward him, one from the origin of the current and the second defiantly from the falls terminating direction of the river.

In that moment of his mind, where thoughts do not yet materialize into verbal potentials, RB still couldn't understand how a boat could have come from where upon his way just traveled from the falls, to his current position, he had seen none.

Quickly RB turned to look at the vessel approaching from upstream and thought to himself, "Most likely another Cauldron Skipper." Both boats appeared to be heading on a hell bent vindictive destructive course. RB considered the boats menacing and he was losing his will to think.

Time slowed to almost standstill for RB, as in somewhat of a fugue he expressionlessly experienced the eminent event. All of a sudden and at the very last moment as Shurlene approached from down current she beat on her steering wheel to avoid a collision with RB. Her boat grazed his as she passed on the right side. Her boat turned rightward and upon half completion of its pass it almost capsized from the rolling angle created by the abrupt turn. In almost perfect unison with her, Medika Mayhem did likewise on the other side of RB's Cauldron Skipper. The passing boats sent RB's sleek Skipper into a jolting and vortextuous motion. He did not know what to think of their wanton and willful recklessness.

6 THE RIVER OF HYPERINFLATION

Medika and Shurlene closed the distance on the water between themselves and RB as his boat had now stilled itself in the water. Medika stood and steered her boat a short distance from RB. Her eyes were locked hatefully upon him. She held this fix on him as she turned and positioned the nose of her Cauldron Skipper at a right angle to the nose of RB's boat.

RB had put a lot of work into this boat and stood proud of his demonstrated ability.

Close to RB, at mooring distance to his boat, Medika held up the fingers of her left hand, palm out, and wiggled her pointed nails in and out in an evil and chaotic motion while she stared at RB's eyes. She was trying to gauge and take the full affect of RB's reaction to her.

Daily, Medika used the two robotic arms with claws on the ends of them to grab and bring up Mucklums from the bottom of the river. In command of her left finger motions the left protruding claw of Medika's boat reached out ever so fast and with a snap like movement bastioned to the anchor eyelet mounted on the front of RB's boat.

Milk Maid Medika Mayhem's face was indeed flush red with anger as she barely managed to spit out these disgruntled words to RB, "You have usurped my Pepper Marley Mayhem," she stuttered a little and continued, "and now what are you doing?" and then again with less stutter and hint of resolve, "What are you doing, making some sort of effort for Tamarack my beloved sister! The gall of YOU!"

Medika then with eyes still on RB, craned her neck out forward a few times as if to say, *"I expect an answer forthcoming right now."*

At the same time Shurlene was holding fast to the gunwale on the other side of his boat and gesturing her index finger in unison with Medika Mayhems words.

Something was welling up in RB, as sensed by Pepper and Helmoot.

Shurlene's boat had an upright mounted hook on a pole that allowed her to safely transfer buckets of Horloff milk from boat to shore and vice versa. It also helped her to get on and off the boat, and served to steady the milk from spilling when underway too. Shurlene took the oversized Horloff milk bucket that was colored white with black spots on it, off her prominently positioned and mounted shepherd's hook, and thrust the darn thing over into RB's Skipper. She then started up the motor of her boat and kept its propeller drive set to neutral. In her cackling tone she commanded to RB, "Provide!"

RB was confused by this demand- Shurlene recognized so and clarified, in her still cackling tone, "Fill my bucket!"

A queer sense of apprehension started to overtake RB and he heard Shurlene say, "Tamarack!" and then with a more hoarse tone, "Get over here!" Shurlene seeing RB's concern for Tamarack yelled at him, "RB you put Pepper in the bucket RIGHT NOW!" She exhaled the heat from her brain downward through her nostrils and shook her head as she spoke again, "Pepper is a Mayhem as well!"

These two sisters were a lot alike and Medika wanted the attention now. With the dullest and meanest pathetic look on her face that she could conjure up, and in the lowest voice she could summon she said, "Do it now!"

Maniacally she was gleaming as she reached into her pocket and pulled out an oddly fashioned black T bar handled type implement. The business end of it was curly and screw like, as if it was designed for rendering into materials and opening them with a pull. She held up the sharp ended, oddly bent coil, and pointed it at RB. Then clenching the device she turned her wrist left and right, taunting RB. She then spoke these words out of tight frozen lips, "We'll sink you for sure. We'll sink you for sure we will."

"What the hell is that!" RB said seeing the tool.

"It's the last thing seen," Medika replied queerly.

RB turned to look from Medika to Shurlene, who nodded her head at RB in a mocking dumbfounded acting like tone, as if to be in full agreement with Medika.

"They're made for decommissioning, and that's what we intend," croaked Shurlene coolly.

Medika would not let RB ignore her even for a second. Wanting his attention she said with a gutsy tone, "So you like girls, do yah RB?"

RB found himself a little stupefied as he tried to think of how to reply. He started to feel less good about himself.

Medika's evil spirit was given a rush as RB became what she considered to be- uncomfortable. Just when it looked like he had found the presence of mind to answer her; she creaked out, "How would you like lots of hull breaches? Shurlene get your corkscrew too. We've got work to do. Let's see what we can do to this fancy boat."

Anticipating something from Shurlene, RB turned to look. She had her right foot perched up on his gunwale. Her right arm was resting on her right knee and she cried out, "Yah I got one too!"

RB saw her dangling one from her left hand, from a loopy foot long lanyard she held. She swayed it tauntingly, hinting at the harm she could do with it.

Calmly RB breathed deeply and tried to distance himself a little from the situation in an effort to retrieve his sound mind.

He was able to think, at least this much; *"This irrationality should not be occurring,"* and his posture of reality formed with this understanding. His resolve produced a controlling tension in his muscles and he stood taller. Having shaken off the impression and righting his composure he spoke these words, "I see by the travel of your boats that there is some sort of malfunction thereof, I will provide assistance to you as I have to Tamarack." He sought to jar and deny them any reward from their evil posturing and his words seemed to dumbfound Medika and Shurlene who for the first time stared at each other with a unified look of wonderment. Acting like it might be appropriate to say, *"Is this guy for real?"*

After a few moments they shook their unleveled heads, blinked a few times as if to clear their minds of what they just heard and said, "You'll never get it…See these whirl deggiggers, we want to sink this shiny little boat of yours." As they said this, they nodded their heads in unison and patronized him with mocking sympathetic eyes.

RB straightened himself again and said with a lecturing tone, "Judging by your utensils, it appears that an unsafe consumption has been made. At this point maybe it would be best if I take your boats in tow and seeing that yours is already latched on to mine Medika, Shurlene you toss over Mooky Booky's leash and I will tow you also. I have the power."

The two objectionable sisters now mad as all get out and not yet coming to calm, full and peaceful terms spoke, "Let's just get started with our powerful unsafe consumption."

With a cocking motion of her forearm, Medika then pushed a button on the end of her T-Bar whirly deggigger with her thumb, and the coil started to wretchedly spin. Medika then motioned to Shurlene and said, "You do same."

Shurlene then bent over scooped up a little water with her hand and let it coolly trickle through her fingers. She then started her "breach opener" also and stuck it in the water which to her delight churned and spit Cauldron River water this way and that.

 Medika also bent over and reached her implement towards RB's hull all the while looking at him. The tip of her whirly deggigger touched his hull and sparks started to fly wildly in all directions.

It was then that the automatic anti-vandalism protocol on RB's boat started to send out a warning that sounded something like a repetitive reframe, "Bavooney Bundtka, Bavooney Bundt", "Bavooney Bundtka, Bavooney Bundt."

A needle bar on the dial of the anti-vandalism control panel pointed in the direction of Shurlene. A hidden round hatch hole cover opened on the side of RB's hull and a projectile fired from the hole. The projectile had fathom length tether that had a pouch on the end that streamed behind it.

Shurlene was hit with it and yelled, "You Horloff droop!" The projectile end stuck to her on impact. The pouch at the streaming end of the tether exploded open. Billowing forth from them were balloons that rapidly inflated.

As Shurlene's balloon mass was rapidly rising on the tether the needle bar on the round targeting dial pointed at Medika as she was auto targeted. Another hidden round hatch hole cover opened and a second projectile fired. *"Smack,"* the projectile stuck onto Medika and the pouch exploded open with the force of the inflating balloons. She swore frantically and with tight nervous lips, "You son of a Horloff!" while she tried to free herself.

They then started to rise up as they floated in the air. With the audio alarm still booming, they kind of polywobbled about in the wafting air while trying desperately to get a glimpse of RB and figure their new predicament out for themselves.

RB, with a now frantic tone, said "Look what you've done to yourselves; you've activated a smart protocol that I cannot stop. Who knows where you'll end up- the planet Juxpiter perhaps!"

7 COMMISSIONER OF WATERS OLD JOSEY

Pepper and Helmoot's initial gleeful reaction was interrupted upon seeing RB's look of concern. His blank expression showed a sense of righteousness for safety.

Tamarack's eyes were widened as if she was about to cry as she saw her sisters aloft. She turned to RB and said feebly, "They are all I have."

When RB spoke his voice resonated action in course to his crew. To them only a natural leader possessed this capability, and their confidence in him never wavered. Its source developed through reliable responsibility. He could always be trusted and believed by his Moreloafs.

RB felt a sense of empathy but responded in strong voice, "We will save them." He then commanded, "Pepper, Helmoot man the AP!" (AP stood for articulating platform.)

Pepper and Helmoot faithfully raised the targeting platform and manned the sticky gun.

RB commanded again, "Fire on aim and retrieve!"

Pepper and Helmoot worked in unison with Pepper working the crank to turn the AP the gun was mounted on in the target acquisition direction while Helmoot orientated the gun vertically and fired in a vector of anticipation.

As the Sisters rose rapidly in the air the gun spit out projectile after projectile. The projectiles had eel like headed suctions on the ends and leashes that made them retrievable like harpoons.

'***

Meanwhile from down river there approached a former comrade of RB. Why indeed, it was Smokey Josey in his mobile pontoon choir boat christened, "Barnacle Barrier Breaker."

Smokey Josey could see something was amiss and he put both paddlewheels of the "Barnacle Barrier Breaker" into full throttle mode, which propelled the boat just a little faster.

His choir was onboard with him. It consisted of Ms. Randolph, Edora, Ms. Hillsmith and Ms. Bellscooper. They liked to practice singing on the boat, taking short trips and being inspired or influenced in song by the natural environment such as; the fervent green shores and proud rooted trees that had stood for ages and radiated clean air. Smokey Josey then instructed the choir ladies, "Please sing the emergency hymn of waterway safety upon approach. I think that will be appropriate now."

Ms. Randolph summoned herself to initiative and stood in front of the choir. She raised her arms in a rounded upward arc and slowly started to sing the first word, giving the rest of the choir time to synchronize together on the first word, "Oh...."

> "Oh little boat upon the sea.
> Won't you please get home safely?
> Oh sailors in times of great misery.
> We stand proudly for thee.

Oh winds of now Great Decree.
Won't you calm for wee.
Oh waves of great degree.
Please settle down quickly.
Oh shipmen flown into the sea.
Please find dry ground readily."

It was just then, at the last verse, of the choir's prayer in song, that a sticky arrow struck its course and nailed one of the wafting miscreants.

Medika howled, "Ow!" and then, "Son of a Carpetti!" Upon the arrows first impact, the audio boom from RB's Skipper reduced to half its full level and Medika's rapid ascent was brought to a halt, when the slack in the tether diminished.

Ms. Randolph instructed again and raised her arms to start the first word or note of the song, as you will. Strengthened by their resolve and seeing Shurlene rapidly escaping out of range the choir belted their song out even more.

"Oh little boat upon the sea.
Won't you please get home safely?
Oh sailors in times of great misery.
We stand proudly for thee.
Oh winds of now Great Decree."

Helmoot keened up his eye as much as possible while diligently taking final aim as the sticky arrow reservoir was just about depleted. The choir did not waiver;

"Oh sailors in times of great misery.
We stand proudly for thee.
Oh winds of now Great Decree…"

The penultimate arrow indeed faithfully stuck onto Shurlene and she yelled, "You Mothers Damned Rock Head." The audio alarm faded to zero.

Both Medika and Shurlene could now be readily retrieved but they were still in no mood to be chastised.

Luckily the Barnacle Barrier Breaker was nearing and Smokey Josey hollered out boisterously, "How can me and the choir be of assistance?"

"There has been an error of judgment here today and I would appreciate it if you could take the reins of these two wonderful ladies that we have rescued from peril, of their own source and doings and see to their safe descending," RB said.

8 THE FURTHER ACQUAINTMENT OF RB AND TAMARACK

"You can stay here with Old Josey and wait for your sisters, but you're welcome to come along with me," RB said to Tamarack.

Seeing Tamarack's eyes were sad and longing RB held out his hand and she took it and then hugged him. The two, now through odd circumstances a pair, were on their way again. Not counting his two loyal sidekicks who snuggled to the sides of the hull in the bow while they rested.

Feeling awkward about what happened, RB was the first to speak, "Well this has been quite a day, but aside from all the commotion there was beautiful weather today." He continued more serious and to the point, "I know your boat meant a lot to you. I will do everything I can to help you. I would like to be there for you."

Tamarack replied, "I can always get a new boat. I owe my life to you RB. RB I want to say something to you. I know you're some years older than I." She stuttered a little and then regained her speech, "I've watched you since I was a little girl. I have always liked you." She then looked at him with sad eyes.

RB not knowing what to say spoke, "My heart throbs for you now." Upon seeing her mutual confirmation response RB continued, "Please come and join me by my side."

Tamarack responded with eyes aglow, but they were pointed downward as she did not want to reveal her anticipation, and joined him on the bench seat.

With his right hand still on the steering wheel RB reached over with his left and embraced her. He gently pulled her close to him. She sighed and rested her head on his shoulder. She was breathing deeply, almost like a cooing bird.

RB started singing to her softly, "Today was a beautiful day. My darling, you made it that way."

"I love you more than words can say. Look over on the shore, at that beautiful Birds Jay."

Not wanting to be bested Tamarack chimed in, "Oh that beautiful Birds Jay. Well I have some words to say. I have loved you from the day I first saw you."

At this point Pepper and Helmoot's feet started a tapping to the sound of her words. Along the shore a bird with a red and gold shield like symbol on its wing, commonly known as a Speacherfrinde, puffed up its chest and preened its feathers in the gentle winds. It started singing too while stepping from one paddle foot to the next on a branch.

A Paddlequack, a swimming type of bird was standing on a rounded rock near shore too. It started cantilevering from one foot to the other in what seemed to be in unison with the two lovers joined through circumstance.

"Your presence completes me. The way you look at me now- I've been longing for and how. Don't bother about my sister the Horloff or the other the Mucklam. I want you to know who I truly am."

After the moments of passion and romance in song, they were just content to be silent with the moment. The forested shores too, seemed to glimmer with a rich and enchanting green, as if the aura of their love was imparted to them. The river water seemed in transition to an eased placidity and it could not be denied that the harmony that had been created between these two in love had changed the physical realities via expanding transformations of betterment. Their love having created an unknown idealism that manifested itself through a representation in the physical world.

After a little while RB took his eyes off the river and just gazed at Tamarack who was snuggled closely to his left side. When their eye's met it was as if their two souls had become one. Next to him she seemed peaceful and warm. She too, felt comfort in being near to him- his strength and breathed calmly as if the intimacy she felt with him was a realization of her life's goal. She felt she regained her sense of innocence from when she was young and unaware of her sisters' brash dealings. The short moment was an eternity to RB and Tamarack- all he knew to do was to kiss her. And at that moment he did.

Her favorable response was more than he expected, and this led to them kissing and caressing each other heatedly. So much so that RB reached back and shut off boats motors without leaving her lips.

Pepper and MSSR put their front paws down in front of them on the deck and rested their heads while they sneaked squints at the entangling closeness of RB and Tamarack.

9 MEDIKA AND SHURLENES FLAMING MAD REVENGE

Meanwhile, Medika and Shurlene, stuck aloft on the retriever cords, were able to summon back their angry composure. Medika stared at Shurlene with her best bully boy look, long enough to catch Shurlene's attention. Medika gave Shurlene the, *no word's*, signal of the index finger over the lips and then pointed down to Josey's boat. Shurlene in return looked at Medika with a vindicating expression that was frozen on her face. Upon recognizing that she had the command of Shurlene, Medika started to discreetly pull herself hand over hand down to the boat her retriever cord was bastioned to. Shurlene followed in manner.

While Medika was still held ten feet buoyant in the air above the deck of the boat, she pulled out her hull decommissioning screw and popped her inflated suspending "restraint". Medika landed on deck her face beat red with anger. With a quick swoop of her retriever cord she lassoed all of the choir; Ms.

Randolph, Edora, Ms. Hillsmith and Miss Bellscooper, around their legs.

With another sharp pull she sent the choir off balance at their knees. In a throaty gruff tone she then insulted, "You sing with the fishes now." With a running pull of the cord by Medika they were sent into the water of the Cauldron River. The otherwise proper contrite Ms. Randolph was heard with a swearing tone, "You won't get away this!" Edora swam to the surface and wiped her wet hair from in front of her face and looked in horror.

Shurlene was now on deck of Old Joseys boat too, she took her sharp hull breaching screw and cut out a long section of retrieving cord from that which was attached to her.

She caught Old Josey from behind with the rope and wrapped it around his neck. Quickly then she tied the rope so that it formed a loose collar loop that she could use to control him with.

Medika then levered the Old Josey's boat, the "Barnacle Barrier Breaker," to full throttle so none of the choir splashing about in the river could scramble back aboard. The Barnacle Barrier Breaker was moored to both the Mooky Booky and Medika's Cauldron Skipper, and they traveled along in tow.

Shurlene using the collar she had formed around Old Josey's neck to hold him in submission brought him to his hands and knees. Shurlene then said to Old Josey, "We're going for a little walk to my boats now, where yours is goings I've got's no ways of knowings."

Shurlene wrangled Old Josey into her boat and tied him off to her milk maid hook and then went to full throttle.

Medika, her co-imprint, ran and leapt into her own Skipper. There she saw Ms. Hillsmith who had just climbed aboard and was sopping wet. Ms. Hillsmith pointed her finger at Medika as if to start to lecture but before she could speak, with one roundhouse blow to the jaw, she was knocked into the Cauldron River by Medika. "Sing about that!" Medika voice scorned to Ms. Hillsmith who then wailed in tears.

With tow line from Josey's boat still attached she put her boat to full throttle and with chaotic control banked left. She did a one hundred and eighty degree turn and jackknifed into the side of old Josey's boat. With a good riddance motion she raised her arm. The hull breaching screw still in hand she quickly snapped the towline with a chopping motion. She looked back once again at Ms. Hillsmith and vetted these words with scowl, "You're done singing!" The motors of Medikas boat were then brought to full breath.

Medika and Shurlene were underway and setting to get a good fix on RB again. Stride for stride in the river current the two boats made their hell bent swarm to RB!

As the two boats neared RB's once more, RB's boat initiated anti-saboteur protocol again and sent out air buoyant based projectile launched restraints. But as the stickum projectile, tethered at the end of a cable, fired at Medika she raised her hull breaching screw in defense. The stickum bastioned onto her screw per her intention. She in turn swung it around overhead enough times to build momentum and flung it at the side of RB's hull by the waterline, where fuel containment reservoir was located. The stickum stuck to his hull- all the while the breaching screw still turning. The breaching screw coiled and then caught at the side of RB's hull. The rotary motion of the hull breaching screw drilled a hole through the primary hull, the secondary hull and then through the fuel tank.

"Pepper, Helmoot tuck yourselves in the bow," RB commanded, and the Moreloafs complied.

Mockingly Shurlene did, what she considered to be, a fancy two step dance and thereby stepped aside of the "harpoon" that was launched at her. As the stickum harpoon passed by her, with the potentiating balloon streaming behind it a short distance, she grabbed hold of the stickum ended harpoon at its midsection and then yelled, "RB you menace!" Quickly and carefully she reached just behind the stickum part so that she didn't get stuck and did what she thought was another fancy little two step over to Old Josey and affixed the stickum end to the skin of Old Josey's back. Old Josey then started to rise up into the air on the buoyancy of the inflating balloon. He was in great danger as he was still tied off to Milk Maid's boat hook via the prior doings.

To RB, Shurlene said, "It appears we have unfinished business. You give us Pepper Mayhem and Tamarack and we'll trade you Old Josey here."

"Time is running out," Medika chimed.

Tamarack seeing the predicament that formed, said to RB, "Don't worry RB I'll be all right," and then leapt into Medika's boat.

"Come aboard Pepper!" Medika commanded but Pepper wasn't budging.

Seeing that Old Josey's life was in danger RB said to Pepper, "You better go." At which point Pepper reluctantly jumped into Medika's boat too. Somewhat as promised Shurlene cut the line holding Old Josey by the neck to her boat hook, but she did not free him from the inflated restraint and Old Josey floated up and away from the boats.

Medika lit up her tangleweed smoking pipe and with a mocking stare looked at RB and said, "And another thing... Get!" Holding the same evil stare she emphatically dropped the still lit lighting stick in the prismatic fuel slicken water off the back of RB's Cauldron Skipper boat. The surface alit in a poof of noise. Medika looked enraged as the flames of the dangerous burning fuel slick chased towards RB's fuel tank.

To inform RB of what was to happen RB's command and control center then bellowed a quick uni-syllable audio stream, "Heuristically-determined-safety-protocol-formation-initiated-RB-hang-on." The ignition to the drives of the boat were started by the boat itself, its command module that is, and sent the Skipper to full throttle in the direction of the falls. RB reasoned why, *"It is commencing this action in order to more quickly free itself from the flames by avoiding collisions with the two boats that might have allowed the flames to catch up with the Skipper, as it's travel was likely to be inhibited by the other boats."*

Medika and Shurlene were now high on evil. Medika threw over a long rope to Shurlene and yelled, "Quick release tie it to your moor at length. We're going to corral him over." They looked at each other and then ahead as they accelerated at the same speed and gave maniacal chase again. Catching up with him they started to channel his boat in between theirs. One on each side, they were bumping him, in order to keep him on a straight and direct course to the falls.

"Don't do this Medika," Tamarack said and ran and grabbed her by the arm.

"We know what's best around here," Medika scolded and pushed her down. Tamarack almost fell out of the boat.

"Don't interfere again," Medika said to her little sister.

"Everything seems to fall just into place for you don't it? Here is where you fall into place!" Shurlene screamed as they had driven him close and fast to the falls. They pulled on the ends of the quick release knots of the rope, that bound their boats, and each veered off to its own respective side.

At the last moment RB commanded Helmoot, "Abandon ship!" and the faithful Moreloaf did so. But it is too late for RB.

As RB's boat rocketed over the falls, command and control voiced to him, "Initial fuel tank hull shock lessening, initiating double hull Horloff foam sealant containment release procedure." The expanding chemical resistant foam was released between hull layers and then spewed out from the hole of the hull breach, as if smoking puffs from a tangleweed pipe.

10 THE WORBLER RESCUE

Helmoot could not escape the force of the current upon impact and a cracking noise was heard as Helmoot met with the rocks at the base of the falls. RB and his boat were propelled further forward in the air as he had rocketed off the falls before crashing. Accordingly they were adrift and unfortunately they were separate. RB was knocked unconscious- and is now subject to the free floating manner of the current.

RB's life preserving jacket had been designed with a type of buoyancy that defied the gravity of water. The space in the jackets layer was created to have a dynamic that made it seem bigger and lighter than it was, a super lightness not of gas but of anti-water. A repelling reaction created in the water kept water at a distance from the surface of the jacket; the form of the repelling action can only be termed respect for a property of nature that encompassed the incarnate being of RB in his jacket. The captive power of the jacket, or the way it held onto RB's upper body was accomplished by a fiber orientated and sewn into horizontal channel like stripes. Submerged in water the vein like fibers in the suit hardened to form a semi encapsulating ribbed structure, so that it did not matter if the front of the jacket was fastened or not. The form made in conjunction with wearing it over the arms created a captive jacket that also held RB buoyant in the water. His jacket also took in rays of the sun and stored them, thereby creating a power source for the field that repelled water to some distance from itself. The opposing displacement of water provided buoyancy. It was almost as if the jacket exuded an oily Horloff slick but the technology, as described, was far different from that. Floating in such a manner with the jacket on, his feet provided the ballast that kept him upright with his head above water.

The slowly passing shores were somewhat quiet and a sad aura permeated the scenery as RB was carried face up downstream with the serenity of nature. Time passed as he floated; his spirit somewhat between heaven and Aqua Caverness, with the heavens reflecting mournfully on this man's previous struggle for life.

'***

Somewhere far from here, downstream, Beesil Worbler, one of the Sesame Worbler race beings, sensed a calling. Something', an inkling of emotion in her heart, then commanded her actions. Without telling anyone, she mounted into her subsurface cruiser and set it to autopilot- maximum upstream thrust.

The Sesame Worblers were a bumpy walking short species. The tops of their heads looked like they had a white hive as a hat but it was really part of them. They were strong, humble and sweet; in summary a good natured race of people.

After a certain distance Beesil Worblers autopilot disengaged and her control system announced, "Unchartered territory encountered.   Advised manual control with navigational computational systems aid."

Beesil Worbler then felt that something in her heart was guiding her to be stronger.   Contemplatively she rubbed her hands together and adjusted herself to a serious posture.   She then grabbed hold of the reins so to speak; the reins being a double pistol gripped steering mechanism of her subnaught. Subnaught was the name for a submersible nautical craft capable of holding one person.

She then spoke to her vessels command center, "Engage course plotting, tracking, vectoring and recording mode.   Make special annotation of any near passing hazards."

With a focus of concentration that could not be broken, the diminutive little being piloted the waterway effortlessly.   With a down to business type expression on her face that was supported and driven by a welling of her being, she thought to herself, "May God be the fear, I've got good to do."

Time transformed and lessened to her on her dead fast journey.   The subnautical boat and her became one as they traveled what seemed to be endlessly, on her yet unsure quest. Somehow it was as if her speed and purpose created a temporal shift, thereby what made her heart grow stronger was drawing her towards here in the world.

Instinctively Beesil Worbler slowed her subnaught and raised it to full surface mode.   She saw him floating in the water.   Without reason his face was distinctly familiar to her. She felt she knew him at the level of their souls- as if their essence of being had thought peacefully together in the same permisphere.

Beesil Worbler opened the hatch to her subnaught and held RB to the side of it.   She prayed, "Be well beautiful one, be well beautiful one," to the waterlogged boat racer.

When she felt the warmth of his soul present she activated communications and sent the urgent homing signal message to her Villa Settle, "MOB found adrift and unconscious at coordinate vector stream, hmv453, vy63572183, vx43756142. Navigational data stream data sent requesting Glommerate-Expo-Speed Support immediately."

The distress call is heard at Sesame Worbler Villa Settle. Immediately a fleet of Sesame Worbler pilots pulled on their one piece rescue uniforms, first up over their feet, they then tucked their arms in their sleeves and with one motion bundled their watertight front flaps. They were readied for a perilous rescue. The suits bore the emblem of a custom compass rose.

They scrambled into their subnaughts and fired up the immediate response engines. Piloting their subnaughts they then streamed out onto the surface of the river from the thick brush lined shore. Each pilot maneuvered their respective vessels into tight proximity to one another and they submerged.

The echelon formation was creating a unified hum that started to resonate. They watched their instrument panels tentatively as the resonance built on their gauges. The echelon leader then voiced on the com system, "Prepare for subnaught combination and integration." He continued, "Countdown commencing in three, two, one. Engage automated proximity guidance system."

At this point the ten Sesame Worbler subnaught crafts joined together to create a Glommerate-Expo-Speed-Structure. The echelon commander then gave her final commands before attaining Glommerate-Expo-Speed, "Entering navstream data of received transmission into piloting system. Engage individual navigational release controls sequentially." She watched the instrument panel as echelon Worblers two through ten switched to echelon commander based control. When they completed she voiced, "Initialization structure sequence complete, engaging Glommerate-Expo-Speed on my countdown; two, one, on." With Glommerate-Expo-Speed switched on she commented rhetorically, "Fore water gasification vacuum created, aft reconstruction enabling. Hang onto your seats!"

The unified resonance now started to pulsate. The pulsate propulsion creating a fore vacuum which pulled the GESS through the water. The super craft ripped through the water with the locomotive power of a jagged bolt of lightning, as water was turned into gas in front of the GESS and then reconstructed back to water aft of the GESS.

Soon after, the echelon commander of the Worbler GESS then voiced, "Disengaging GESS upon reaching computational arrival coordinate. Attempting contact with Beesil Worbler....GESS to Beesil Worbler we have arrived and are surfacing, awaiting retort and visual confirmation of location."

"GESS, this is Beesil Worbler transmitting current coordinate vector."

GESS commander then replied to Beesil, "CCV received, ETA in three, two, one."

11 TAMARACK'S SEARCH

Medika now had Tamarack and Pepper in her boat. Looking in the direction of the falls she momentarily paused with Shurlene to share the look of delight in the terminal destruction of RB.

Medika turned her boat upstream and Tamarack then screamed in protest, "What have you turned into! What if he is still alive? I knew you were evil, but murder!"

Medika in her cat river slang mocked any care one might have for his life, "What if he, who he, ain't alive?" and turned up the throttle.

Tamarack; distraught and helpless to the controlling will of her older sister- sat and wept, while Pepper winced and Medika leered. Indeed, Medika was shaking, as she was happily possessed by the evil she conjured from her crime. Seemingly she had never been happier in her life. After awhile she gleefully said to Tamarack, whose face was stripped of emotion in abject terror, "It will be nice to have Pepper around the house again. Tamarack, as soon as we get back you takes a dusting stick to my place to celebrate her return and have things nice for her."

At which point Tamarack sobbed even more loudly.

When they got home Tamarack grabbed the dusting stick and started to sweep. She waited until Medika was out of sight, at which time she snuck out the door and headed for Cherry Bo Berries place.

In an agitated state she rapped on the door. When Cherry Bo Berry opened Tamarack frantically spewed out these words, "Medika and Shurlene sent RB over the falls. We have to go and look for him. We have to get help, they're out of hand. He could still be alive. We could save him. At the very least let me borrow your Skipper."

"Calm down, we'll go right away," Cherry Replied. Cherry then gathered a coat and a bag of gear from the boathouse and they embarked in Cherry's Cauldron Skipper in an effort to save RB.

Cherry too, looked distraught as she piloted the craft.

Cherry drove the nose of her Cauldron Skipper up onto the shore just before the falls and tied it securely to a tree. And the two disembarked and made their way down the steep rocky slope that skirted the river to the base of the falls.

"I don't see any sign of him or his boat," Cherry said as she gandered the immediate area.

"He may have swam to shore or washed up still breathing further down, we'll have to keep going," Tamarack said.

They made their way through unpathed territory. Further downstream Tamarack found a shoe washed up in the shore brush, "It has to be his. That's his distinct compass rose insignia on the outer side."

"That is identifiably his as I have never seen another like it. He might still be alive. He was wearing his jacket, the one that turns into a float."

"Oh be hopeful for him Cherry. I fell in love with him."

And with renewed sense of hope after finding his shoe, Cherry and Tamarack kept searching.

'***

Meanwhile Helmoot was lying on his side, not too far in distance downstream from where Cherry and Tamarack were looking for RB. Helmoot was wincing in pain from the force of the fall and distraught because he was separated from his master. He had sought to swim after RB to save him but could not keep up because of his injury. Helmoot turned his attention to a rustle in the brush and found the resolve to tense up his weakened body muscles to ready himself for any oncoming confrontation. He turned to face the nearing sounds and tuned his ear muscles some to listen. Through what he sensed then, he knew distinctly, *"It is Tamarack and Cherry Bo Berry approaching!"* and this put him at ease.

'***

Upon making their way through a series of some more shore brush they found Helmoot lying on his side- breathing deeply and whimpering.

Helmoot barked out softly, "I have been searching for RB after I could not save him. This is as far as I could get with my paw."

Seeing the hurt paw Tamarack focused her concern on Helmoot and assured, "You're going to be alright. We'll bandage you up and get you to safety."

Helmoot bemoaned, "I got this far with no sign of him, but something strange happened here. I'll show you what I saw and I'll do it with my paw." At which point Helmoot held his broken paw, warm from fever, to Tamarack's calf.

Tamarack looked as if she was seeing inside her own head and said, "In my mind's eye I see a light streak under water-what does it mean Helmoot? Do you think it was RB's Skipper under water or someone with a search light came and helped him? And how did you make me see that?" Tamarack asked.

"It's part of my team training. I sense RB is alive Tamarack," Helmoot replied.

Hearing the good news Tamarack's empathy shifted again to Helmoot and she said, "Helmoot we have to get you medical attention. Ms. Hillsmith is good at doctoring, we'll see if we can find her."

'***

When Tamarack got back to Up Falls she went immediately took Helmoot to Ms. Hillsmith and Helmoot is wrapped in bandages that hardened like a shell.

After she saw that Helmoot would be okay she stormed over to her two evil sisters place and said, "Shurlene, Medika, I can't live here with you anymore. Cherry has an extra room at her place and that is where I will stay until I find someplace good of my own."

12 THE DECADENT SOIREE

Medika and Shurlene were sitting together on their couch. They celebrated what they each considered to be a personal victory, by gorging themselves on Mucklums and Horloff cream.

Medika throatily groaned, "Sis that was sure some day," and slapped Shurlene on the thigh.

"We sure did the river up right." Shurlene replied.

As they sat Medika was symmetrical to Shurlene with her left leg perched on the lounge table and her right leg in an open direction of body language to Shurlene.

The classless and crass tone of Medika's voice is next to be heard, "Did you see the look of horror on Josey's face as he floated away above the trees?"

"What a guy!" Shurlene spake.

The events of the day had rejuvenated the evil old hag's spirits' as they acted and thought themselves as rulers of Aqua Caverness.

Medika laughed like she ran a brothel and said, "Now we'll have things more our way around here."

Unhappy to be with them Pepper was lying on the floor in resentment. They readily mistook their commiserating company with one another for delight. They were absent of conscience for their actions. The evening one dreadful nasal laugh or jeer after another.

Medika continued, "Who did he think he was defying us with his life for so long. We don't have to look at him anymore!"

Shurlene motioned to Pepper who was panting with nervous shallow breaths, "Come here darling. It is so good to have you in your proper home again. Come here Pepper." Pepper did not respond so Shurlene wretchedly bellowed out a command, "PEPPER COME TO MAMA NOW!"

Pepper still did not obey so Shurlene got to her stout feet and grabbed her by the collar and brought her to sit on her lap.

Shurlene said to Pepper sitting on her lap "Isn't it good to have Pepper back again. Give mamma a kiss. Oh yes give mamma another kiss. Oh you're a good Moreloaf, you are. Yes, give another kiss. Oh you taste so good, you do. Yes, now you give Medika a kiss too. Yes. Now don't be shy you. No. No. You don't be so shy. Here you go Medika."

Medika petted Pepper profusely and said, "Oh now, you give auntie Medika a kiss too. Yes, you like to kiss yes Auntie Medika don't you? Yes, those are tears of joy you are crying aren't they?"

13 WORBLERS RESCUE OF THE BOAT

RB started to move his head slightly, and it appeared as if he was gaining consciousness. He slowly opened his eyes and found unfamiliar surroundings. The first words he uttered were, "Where am I?" followed by "Who are you?" and mumblings of, "Tamarack and my boat..."

"Rest easy," Beesil said to RB. "You are with friends now. We will care for you until you are well. You had quite a scrape."

Beesil Worbler spoke to RB in soft humming like tones that to rose and fell melodically, "I am the team rescue leader, Beesil Worbler. I am of the Sesame Worbler tribe. I was on long range reconnaissance and spotted you floating unconscious in the river. I sent a distress call to dispatch a full rescue team. You are in a temporary emergency chamber, TEC for short, created by temporarily combining several ships together as one. We have given you first aid support and stabilized your physical being."

She continued, "The treatments we have provided will gradually make your wholeness of being revitalized. But you must be patient. We have given you orally administered vital drips and top coat life healing infusioms. These treatments were designed for the life system of your body. They are sought after naturally by your biological repair processes. In effect, they enrich your body's life systems at an accelerated rate without any degradation to bodily integrity. In actuality they will now combine with your body's systems resulting in a more robust longevity. As to your boat I have spoken with the echelon commander that piloted this GESS. Your vessel has been located and the commander has been posted with it. Multi-array scans reveal what appear to be structured integrity breaches and some drive system deformations. I have requested a transport squadron to recover the craft. Mass density infraspection reveals it is within our capability. Six RTS subnaughts are waiting to be given the go ahead upon our eminent arrival to Villa Settle."

After the hum line of words RB's vision was starting to clear and he was becoming more coherent. Upon scanning Beesil he said, "You are wearing my emblem?"

"I have given you too much information for you to absorb already. It is best that you rest for awhile. More of our nature will be revealed to you when you are better." Beesil is interrupted by an announcement emanating from her systems control panel, "Disengaging GESS drive, ETA... Villa Settle reached."

Hearing this Beesil immediately activated the public address system control interface and spoke, "This is Beesil Worbler we have arrived with the M.O.B. Launch second GESS fleet to retrieve damaged watercraft."

14 BACK TO HEALTH

RB awakens and finds himself in a cozy cabin. The view from the window was one of forest trees. The peaceful scenery lifted his spirits immediately. He suddenly noticed miniature Worblers watching him as they were perched on a bench to his left. As he looked at them, what he presumed to be Worbler children, they smiled at him and he thought, "They look like greedy little bandits."

One got up and waddled to the door and opened it. He then stuck his head out and announced, "He's awake."

"What are your names?" RB asked.

One of the Worbler children looked at the other two and mustered the most stern look she could. She then pointed at RB and said, "We are bandits here to steal your privateer loot." The two other children laughed at this and she continued in a more serious manner speaking, "Now whatever you do, don't flinch. You are not to move. You understand me, you are not to flinch. Don't you dare flinch, not even a little bit!"

RB interrupted this display by saying, "Maybe you could find me your most senior bandit?"

The outspoken Worbler ran over to RB, pinched his big toe, and ran out of the room. The other two patted his foot also, and scurried out the door in a hurry.

RB thought, *"Maybe I could have flinched,"* but he realized that his bones were still aching some and therefore that he shouldn't try to rise to his feet.

After a little while there was a knock on the cabin door. Calmsy Worbler appeared and spoke, "Good morning Royal Barron, my name is Calmsy Worbler. We have been awaiting your arrival. You are known to us through permispherical means. I hope the children did not bother you too much. You can consider them curious admirers." Five children then entered into the cabin behind Calmsy, three of them he has knowledge of.

Calmsy continued, "Royal Barron you're a hero and inspiration to us every day. Now it is time for your morning revival hymn." At which point she turned to the innocent faces of the Worbler choir members and did an altogether movement with her arms as if she were conducting the opening of a symphony. The Worbler children then started to sing in tones and harmonies that blurred RB's comprehension.

"Royal Barron of the river.

Your heroics make us shiver.

Be well soon a great man broken.

God's love for you is yet unspoken.

For when thee have regained your being.

A great journey you will be seeing.

You will travel far to your homeland.

And give tokens to the sand.

For now, you must know.

We regret the day you decide to go.
For we treasure you here with us.
Now go to the bathroom and piss out some puss."

At which point the children scurried out of the room.

Calmsy then spoke, "I will keep you company for awhile, for I would to adore your smile."

"You call me Royal Barron...why?"

"If RB does not stand for Royal Barron, what does it mean?" Calmsy asked.

"Royal Barron it is then," answered RB.

She continued non-lyrically, "I have some breakfast for you in this satchel." From which she proudly pulled out a covered sectional dinner plate and rested it on the table beside his bed. Eagerly she awaited his reaction.

He first tried what looked like wood shavings. To him they were crunchy and tasted kind of bitter. They readily liquefied in his mouth but had more of a smooth finish after he swallowed. The flavor then indeed made RB salivate.

"What do you call this part?" he asked.

Calmsy thought for a second and replied, "The technical name for it is Coboconulous Salvatorous.

He then tried some green curly grass like stuff that had steam rising from it, and it had a tart taste. He noticed a different flavor too; in the midst of the savory gravy coating it had.

"The technical name for that is Sprouticulous Nutriculous," Calmsy eagerly offered as she was proud of the meal.

On the left side of the plate was what looked to be a patty of meat to him. It had an orange and yellow swirling mix of gravy covering it. RB ate some and asked, "And that was?"

Calmsy replied, "Beanulous Proteinulous. But you can alternatively think of it as termed Patty Oh Bean. The sauce as you know it is a fruiticolous citriculous preparation."

To wash down all that food RB was given a drink from a metallic mug. It had a lid that was attached to the top of its handle by a lever so that it could be readily closed to keep the liquids inside it fresher. Calmsy now quite proficient added, "What you are drinking now is called Hormiculous Rooticulous cider. It is soothing good for your internals."

As if she tasted the words on the tip of her tongue she continued, "In the other cup you will find Nonparticulous Ubiquitous." She nodded her head a few times, "I mean water."

After eating the food and drink RB seemed more relaxed than ever, the aches he had upon awakening were lessened.

"I think I need to use the bathroom," he said. RB moved to sit on the edge of the bed. In a few moments he was able to gain enough circulation in his body to stand upright and did so. He then eased his way to the bathroom.

'***

RB underwent many weeks of treatment- the Worblers teasing him in the morning. Until one day it was different and RB gathered his things together just before the time that the Worblers usually came in early in the morning.

He had made it look like he had left and for when the Worblers entered.

"He is gone, he has left us!" a small Worbler said with tears in her eyes.

The rest of the morning Worblers looked around with vacant faces as if to say, *"He can't be gone!"* and they too started to cry.

"I wouldn't leave without saying goodbye," RB said as he appeared from the doorway to the washroom, his face had a genuine loving smile on it.

Upon seeing him they started to sing;
"Oh Royal Barron of the flowing sea.
How we love to be with thee.
Matter not our frightful presence.
Consider it an offhand blessence.
Take good heart in what you eat.
 Cooking for you is a pleasure feat.
 It is time for you to see our settled Villa's.
 You greedy eater of Minchilla's.
 As you think of what's to happen.
 We will take joy in your revamping- when your feet a start a stamping."

RB then joined them in their intricate choreographed Worbler dance, where three led him this way, while one snuck behind and patted him on the bottom. He looked to see who passed on by, but there was no one seen by his rightful eye.

"Your transformation to a better being.
Is something you will be seeing.
You will pedal onto powered stars.
And know elaborately of things called cars.
You will stand always for what is right.
And give weakened minds great insight.
You will travel day and night.
And win the heart of a girl that you found right.
Inspiration could be your middle name.

As the fight for good your claim to fame."

RB spent that day walking around the Villa Settle. He found himself sitting by the water's edge. As he watched the crystal clear water slowly flowed by he thought, *"The circumstance of my going over the falls was no accident. My father was said to have mysteriously gone over the falls too. Good people back home probably don't know what happened to me. I have a duty to the community, to tell of what the sisters did, so that no one else will be endangered by them. And Tamarack is not like her older sisters. She being the youngest was influenced by them. She loves me and I am attracted to her, in fact I love her. I need to protect her from her older sisters too! As much as I love it here with the Sesame Worblers I must repair my Cauldron Skipper and journey home."*

'***

The next morning RB was awoken by the sound of the Worblers singing.

"Awaken now big Ouhgerstone.

For you should see the sun hath shone.

It delivers life to land.

And food we pick with loving hand.

At the end of the day you must not escape.

The shadow cast on this great landscape.

For have hope in brightness for tomorrow.

And be not set with greatness sorrow.

We have seen you at the helm of greatest ship.

Racing about in frantic clip.

Now of Rooticulous cider have another sip."

RB went for a walk that day to get his strength back.

'***

The next morning as RB awoke he saw that Beesil was with the Worblers and he heard them sing;

"Awaken oh flashy one.
 For if not now you miss the sun.
When you finish eating goodness from forest floor.
Leave the tray on by the door.
Then jump up and down and get things moven.
He who could get just fat in hooven."

Each of the young ones patted him on the foot and exited.

"Won't you join us for dinner at our outside tables tonight?" Beesil asked.

"I would love to."

RB spent this day regaining his strength.

'***

"Glad you could join us," said Beesil as RB joined them for dinner at the long table.

"Thank you for inviting me."

"You Worbler's sure do know how to cook. You won't believe me but I remember all the flavors that Calmsy Worbler told me about. And I can tell just what you have added to these green grain bowls to make them taste good!" RB said as he tasted a fork full of the dish in front of him.

"I didn't show you all the good cooking," Calmsy said quickly after RB spoke.

"Well I sure learned a lot from what I remember."

"Mannersbee you will," Beesil said to the younger Worblers who had trouble sitting still at the table, "Mannersbee you will!"

"Ust's more important's of knowledge speak now," Borled Bab added.

"Tell us how you came drifting down current?" Beesil asked.

"Two sisters, of the settlement where I live, got angry at me while we were boat racing and ran me over the falls."

"Why do you think they did this?"

"I don't know why they got so angry, but I think it had something to do with rain of spheres," RB said.

"What do you mean by rain of sphere?"

"On a clear day I was sitting in my boat and strange energy spheres rained from the sky. They hit the water next to my boat with a splash. They seemed to possess intelligence. I examined them; they were each about this big." RB cupped his hands to form a bowl. "They were harmless. I stowed them in my boats reservoir and they changed shape and color and infused themselves into my boats motors."

"Did they look good to eat?" asked Borled Bab.

"I never considered it," replied RB.

"Why not?"

"They were friendly and pet like. Have you ever heard of such things as this?" RB asked.

"I have not heard stories of such."

"I think they helped my boat race faster."

"Did they help you win the race the day you went over the falls?"

"I would say they did."

"That means they are on your side," said Cackelton.

'***

The next morning RB awakens to hear the Worblers singing.

"Today you meet red of Ochre.

Who looks like he had too hot a soaker."
A little Worbler said; "You are not allowed to leave.
For my heart, in two, it would just cleave.
It is known only to me that you must stay.
For without you here it would be long day.
If you think you get away.
I fill your boat heap high with hay.
Start your day of peril not of worry.
Nor lest you run in mindless hurry.
May you enjoy all you see throughout your day.
And think of good words to tell of say.
Learn from what on journey pass.
And pray as if in great hall of mass.
Be thankful for the day God given.
And send praise to him for cleanest liven.
Plan for darkness at end of day.
By being proud of what you do and say.
Think well and from your heart give good advice.
Not just once throughout the day but twice and thrice.
This will rid you of great vice.
And melt a heart of what would be ice.
Do not stumble over others feet.
Or envy those whose shoes are neat.
If you hold thoust nose up high.
You will surely get a sty.
He who admire flowers through the day a bunch.
Not be bothered by he with hunch.
It good to hear sound of happy munch.
Followed by dessert of crunch.
Bend thyne metal into curly cue.
As if fashioning a wood some screw.
Think of this as no great chore.

Collect red scraps from minerals shore.
And heat the red hot in the furnace core.
And make to sell at local villa settle store.
And afterwards go find more.
From the stars they came.
And of you we view the same.
Choose carefully what to put and take.
And afterwards clean up with rake.
For here you stay thyne earn your keep.
Take this ax and down with it seep.
Into some lumber from wood heap.
Give thyne strength in this humble manner.
And thyne skin will grow much tanner."

15 BOAT FIXING

RB was nursed back to health by the Worblers and his next task was to repair his boat.

"What kinds of tools do you have to fix things here? Are they ones that I can learn how to use?" RB asked Beesil.

"We have multi material milling means here. And a couple of nice work shop's I'm sure you'll like. Wood Boots Worbler will show you around those facilities and teach you about our machines."

'***

As RB sets to work on fixing his boat Worbler's hide in the periphery and watch him.

"What is he doing?" a young Worbler whispered to another one hiding with him.

"When his boat crashed, rocks must have torn a hole in the side of the hull."

"Shhh. He is crafting form so that he can lay composite material over the top of it to fit in with the contour of the hull," said another older Worbler who crawled up from behind to join them.

"His hands and arms are quite proficient with tools," one Worbler whispered to another as they hid in a separate hiding place from the others.

"A fine craftsman he is," said the other.

RB does not notice the mini Worbler's as they watch him intently.

"Look at his unwavering flow of concentration. It is as if he is mesmerizing the tools in his hands to do the work separate from him."

"His movement's just kind of flow naturally as if there is no wasted energy by him," a peaking Worbler told another.

"Synchronizing his work he is."

RB was working on fashioning a scarf joint, an angled type of end joint, when a queer sense of apprehension came over him and reflexively he looked over his right shoulder. Standing there was a short little beet faced fellow who grimaced at him. RB made eye contact with him and the little man emphatically broke a stick he was holding in his hands. At which point RB said to the elder looking Worbler, "Don't you know distraction is the number one cause of wasteful work and injuries!"

The Worbler closed his eyes, pointed his head down quickly and walked away.

So far RB was able to cut to size wood repair strips for his hull. While he was finishing them to fit in place Beesil Worbler appeared by his side.

"RB what you need to use is a shivums shaver," she said.

"What is a shivums shaver?"

"Here I will show you," answered Beesil.

Beesil walked over to the workbench and found a shivums shaver, an oddly shaped draw type of knife and returned to

RB's side. Sitting next to RB she slowly planed away thin wood strips to what she thought would be a proper fit together.

"Try fitting this piece now," she said.

RB took the strip of wood handed to him and it fit neatly in place to the section that he was repairing.

"Try it," Beesil said as she handed the shivum shaver tool to RB.

RB took long strokes with the shivum shaver and obtained the same results as Beesil had; a perfect fit.

"Thank you," said RB with a smile of gratitude, as he took note of the carefully crafted scarf joints. Beesil went on her way and soon afterward Cackelton appeared on the path by where RB was working on his boat.

"Excuse me Cackelton. Do you have any material of the liquid sort for sealing hulls?" RB asked seeing Cackelton.

Cackelton looked at RB as if he was looking into the distance and spit on his hull. He then raised his left cheek, thereby creating a sneering look on his face.

"You could show a little more respect than that," RB said.

"Try and wipes that off and see what happens," Cackelton chimed.

"I ought to be making you wipe this up or better yet I ought to wipe this up with you!" RB said, ignoring all the Worblers had done for him so far.

Turning away from Cackelton, RB grabbed a nearby rag and upon wiping the insult off he saw the spittle was rapidly forming into a hard shellac like surface.

"That's what we use it for, at least, and your gonna need some more," Cackelton said. Cackelton chuckled and announced aloud to those around, "RB needs more of what he calls hull sealer," Worbler's then emerge and spit shine his hull in a swarm of motion.

"That sure is a nice shiny smooth surface. Thank you," RB said and stood back to admire the hull.

"Would you like us to help right the boat," a Worbler asked.

"Yes that would be very helpful. I had foreseen that I would need to do that soon and did not know who to ask to help. I will stand on the middle of the side and you can stand to the sides of me."

RB stood on the side and Worblers then joined him and grabbed the gunwale of the boat to his sides. "Wait until I give the all together signal, then keep your back straight and lift with your legs." RB looked to his left and right to make sure everyone looked to be in good place and asked, "Everyone ready?"

"Yes we are," said the Worblers.

"Okay lift."

RB lifted and the Sesame Worblers lifted along with him. Some of the smaller Worblers had grimaces on their faces as they raised the boat to the point where their arms were holding the edge straight above their heads. RB and some of the taller Worbler's gave it the final push and it rolled gingerly into the tall grass near the edge of the river so that it was ready to push in the water to float when the time came.

"Thank you very much Worblers. I could not have done that by myself. You don't have to help me anymore now…If I need help I'll know who to ask. Thank you very much."

The Worbler's then went on their merry way except for Cackelton.

"She'll float, but she won't circle an ox bowed moat," Cackelton said in an arrogant manner.

"Now…I have to assess for repairs…to control and propulsion systems. If you would be so kind… I need to concentrate hard while doing this," RB implied to Cackleton.

"Explain to me how you get this thing to move on its own, if you will be so polite?" asked Cackelton.

Seeing that someone was interested in his boats workings RB took the opportunity to explain and started his well-rehearsed favorite diatribe, "The boat is basically powered by hybrid carbon based fuel, with hybrid electric assistance. Each of its two drive shafts contain encompass mounted spherical ball motors. The two motors closer to the prop fire first. As more power is needed, motors on the respective drive shafts and shaft extensions are sequentially engaged. Exhaust is centrically separated in the simple process and fed to subsequent spheres for secondary and tertiary and so on combustion. No emissions are produced. The spheres are coated with thick magnetic plating. Their spherical combustion chamber housings in turn are electro coiled. In effect, all combustion directly drives the shafts, but also charges electro motive drive assists or alternatively is used to crack metered water intake into the gasses of oxygen and hydrogen, which are used in combination with primary combustion source to produce more efficient combustion. This in effect lessens the use of the primary combustion fuel. Spheres can fire in a cross hop pattern whereby sphere number one drive shaft one would be coordinate dependent with sphere number one drive shaft two. Spherical motors and modular driveshaft extensions are in disconnect until throttle is applied. In effect, at full throttle, all sixteen spheres on both drive trains are engaged and as the throttle increases from idle to full mode sphere drives are engaged in a cross hop pattern or stair tooth pattern. If a sharp banking turn were to be made one propeller drive shaft could be disengaged and the parallel one could be firing on all eight spheres in combination with vector directed thrust." RB concluded, "Pretty neat isn't it, all thought of, engineered and produced by myself. I can understand all that- is rather complicated, you might have some questions?"

"That's how ours work too, but not in similar manner," Cackelton replied and promptly spat on part of the aft hull section and said, "You missed a spot."

RB promptly rubbed in the shellac.

Cackelton thought that RB did not think that he understood the drive system and therefore, to show him that he did, Cackleton stated professorially, "If you port in series and biaxially transform the system with tertiary containment chambers, you could produce a venturi drive system which would be quite a bit faster."

"I'm not sure what you mean," RB replied.

"I don't want to sabotage your repair efforts anymore. We have a fellow here that knows more of the skills. He will assist you. His name is Borled Bab Worbler, as a matter of fact he's sitting on top of that garbage container over there. He is one of us but in some way he is not." Cackelton summoned Borled Bad with a motion of his hand.

RB turned to look at Borled Bab as he approached and saw that he was a short little fellow who walked like a Paddlequack. He had noticeable edema in his belly and jowls. He had a little streak of finely greased hair accentuating his otherwise burnish red colored scalp. Except for puffy red flesh and cheeks he resembled the other Worblers.

Borled Bab Worbler swished around some spittle in and between his jowls as he determined if the properties of it were appropriate. One formula of his spittle could eat away metal and the other could make metal temporarily into the consistency of clay.

Borled Bab squatted by the bent propeller and spat on it. The metal propeller then softened slightly and Borled Bab stroked and fashioned it with his fingers and palms. Borled Bab looked carefully at the propeller as it re-solidified. Using his hands as eyes he felt it very carefully. He found a spot on the curve of one blade that he was paying special attention to. He spat on his hands and rubbed the metal where he felt it to be deformed. The metal re-hardened and he quickly felt it and saw that it was okay. He then went to repair the propeller on the second drive shaft.

"The right propeller does not need repair," RB stated.

With a mouthful of spit in cheeks Borled Bab replied, "It needs to be made symmetrical to the more efficient form of shape that I just created."

Borled Bab then spat on his hands and massaged the second prop to a more elongated and trailing tail configuration like he had the first.

"Although not to initial specifications it is more properly articulated and hydro dynamically balanced than it was before," stated Borled Bab with a proud look on his face; that that had become less red.

"Well, thank you very much. I never knew of such type of craftsmanshippings before," said RB.

"Happy to help you out RB," Borled Bab said and went on his way with a confident stride to his walk.

16 RB ROUGH AND THE TRIP HOME

It was time for RB to leave for home. He had come to love the Worblers' who had saved his life and then cared for him. So when it came time to go back home it was a hard thing for him to do. But RB felt a duty to his home community. He was drawn to Tamarack and felt a responsibility to keep her and the others safe from what he knew the two sisters to be. Josey was his friend and helped him when he needed it and Josey was likely to be in danger now.

As he left the cabin he saw that the Worbler's had prepared a big send off for his departure. The whole Worbler community was waiting for him and started singing this song;

> "Royal Barron Rough.
> You're life to us is art.
> The company we shared with you.
> Was a highlight for our crew.
> Don't be a stranger to us here.
> As our love for you is dear.
> Now journey safely home.
> For our hearts with you do roam.
> Continue with courage in the face of danger.

Come to see us in times of trouble.
And if away too long make it here on the double."

It was now RB's turn to give his speech.

RB became sentimental but regained his composure and gave the speech he had prepared;

"Worblers of the river nigh.
You have brought my spirit high.
To meet a people such as you.
Is like a dream of noble true.
You nurtured me when I was ill.
And taught me the work of your mill.
You have raised my faith in fellow being.
Worblers of the land not from seeing.
I will miss you on my journey back.
May the memory of me in your heart never lack.
Beesil I have made a gift for you to keep of me.
It is a model of a boat from sea."

RB handed Beesil the boat and Beesil thanked him, "We will cherish this as we do you. Here is a token to keep you safe. Our image is inscribed inside this clearness stone. It wears like a necklace and creates a goodness zone."

RB put on the necklace and boarded his Skipper while momentarily hiding the tears in his eyes. Beesil said, "We have provided you with provisions for travel and navigational stream data to your point of rescue."

Beesil hugged RB, then another Worbler hugged RB. Then a line formed and every Worbler gave RB a hug including Cackelton and Borled Bab.

RB then got in his Cauldron Skipper, fired up the motors and quietly headed up the river.

Coming from out of nowhere the surface rippled behind RB's boat. From a distance RB saw what looked to be a log like formation on the water's surface. It was accelerating in speed towards RB's Cauldron Skipper.

The Worblers saw it too and sounded the alarm. The otherwise peaceful Worblers were now howling as they looked intently at what was chasing after RB. There were ropes that were tied high in trees. They ran and grabbed the ends of these ropes near the ground and shook the trees to warn RB.

"RB a Surpedo! RB a Surpedo!" they yelled from shore.

Borled Bab ran along the shoreline and launched a spear at the Surpedo.

Seeing and hearing the Worblers fear, RB looked on in horror at what approached and as he did so the linear form broke apart into more than a dozen distinct ripple patterns.

RB smiled and waved to the Worblers, "Do not be alarmed they are *rain of sphere*! They are *rain of sphere*! They are the ionic propensities spinning in the water! It's okay they are rain of sphere. They are spheres that rained; its okay!"

The spheres caught up with RB, popped from the water and propelled themselves through the air to land in RB's boat. RB smiled and waved goodbye to the Worblers on shore. Glancing at the Spheres RB saw that they were brown and did not seem to shine as brightly as they had. *"They no longer seem to possess the strength they first had,"* RB thought in sadness. The spheres then changed from brown to bright green and then faded to a dark green. RB placed them in his secondary reservoir and scooped some water over them. They then turned a brighter shade of green.

"Squadron Alpha commence prepared celebratory departure procession escort," Beesil commanded.

The nine alpha team leaders disembarked in echelon formation. Four subnaughts overtook RB on each side. One submerged behind RB and a few moments later a pop was heard, like a cork from a bottle, as Alpha Team Leader One broke the surface in lead of RB and spiraled through the air like the arc of a rainbow. With a *"plop"* alpha team hit the water, partially submerged and then rose as they gained speed. The four subnaughts on the left converged with the four on the right as they symmetrically wove the surface of the water.

This continued for quite some time until, some distance forward, Alpha team leader pulled to the side of RB's path and stood up in his subnaught. He remained motionless while holding a salute to RB. Alpha team leaders Duce through Ninyo formed consecutively in a single file line behind Alpha team leader. The line of salute formed a closed angle to RB's upstream course.

When RB's approach was parallel with Ninyo, Ninyo stoically saluted. He was followed by Ocho all the way to Alpha Team Leader.

RB returned a salute to each and headed onward.

When RB was out of sight for some time Alpha Squadron commenced their return to their Villa Settle. RB was alone in his journey and quietly contemplated his memory of the Worblers spirit.

'***

RB had traveled for several days when he approached a bend in the river. He looked to the side of his boat to see a Furlucci swimming alongside with him. It quickly scampered onto the flat rocked shore to his right, stood up on its hind legs and put its front paws up in front of its eyes. Then it dove back in the water. When RB saw this he started to think again, *"Lonely days are often filled with short moments of surrealism… in relation to the beauty of nature."*

After the bend in the river there was an entrance to a natural stone walled cavern. RB cut his motors and studied the entrance. He could choose to enter the cavern or fork left on the river. The steep golden face of the water carved stone wall formation was pock marked with birds' nests and the brave roots of Sapscent and White Syrup Bark trees that hung tightly onto its side.

RB consulted the navigational stream maps provided to him by the Worblers and his mind was made up for him. He was to veer right and enter the cavern.

As he entered the dark current of the cavern, beams on the perimeter of his hull illuminated the cavern walls. He saw nests of small driftwood along the sides of the channel and also some stalactite formations of emerald green. The light from his boat lost itself inside the countless refraction's of dazzling green formations. To him this exemplified the beauty of nature, *"A palace of nature,"* he thought to himself. The formations glistened and reflected original hues of green that many would envy the privilege of seeing if given the opportunity.

Unsure of what was to come, he taxied through the cavern at a slow and safe pace in order to maintain his perspective on the walls and the direction of the current. On a bare portion of the cavern wall he saw a drawing of his family's compass rose. Illuminated by the light of his boat he could see that it had been painted with natural pigments. From the way it had aged he could tell it was from a time that long preceded him.

He stopped his boat in order to look at this familiar image for awhile and comprehend its significance. *"It means something. Some kind of connection to history for my family?"* This provided him with a sense of self importance and connection to time that was new to him. And this strengthened his will as he continued his journey through the cavern. He had not gone too much further when he saw that the darkness of the cavern was starting to dwindle. His boat exited the quiet cavern passage into more familiar daylight surroundings.

After a short distance he decided he needed to rest a little. While tying the front mooring line of his boat to a tree at the river's edge, he looked in the shallow water and spotted some Mucklum's. He reached down into the bottom of the river and grabbed a few for lunch.

There were very few trees close to the shoreline and there was a serene beauty in the background of the landscape. He could see a green meadow spotted with yellow flowers that extended some distance inland. As he ate the Mucklums he felt a sense of belonging. This was part of the surrealism he experienced. He contemplated what a nice place it would be to settle.

"Smack," his calm thoughts were interrupted as he picked out the last of the Mucklum meat from the shells with his river knife. He paused to listen. *"Smack,"* he heard it again. It sounded like something flat was clapping against the water's surface. It was coming from around the bend in the shoreline of the river. He would not let this frighten him and turned to look in the direction the disturbance was coming from. *"Smack....Smack,"* he heard it twice more and it sounded to him as if the sound was made with a purpose. He then noticed that something was swimming around some waterlogged trees that were angling up out of the river as the water flowed around and past a shore point. He looked closer and was able to distinguish a Furlucci head as it swam into the main river channel. And then its body was revealed to RB's sight.

"Smack," the Furlucci slapped its broad tail to the calm water surface as if it was demonstrating a showmanship of purpose and form to RB.

'***

After he lunched on the Mucklums and watched the Furlucci swim, he drifted off to sleep and started to dream of being in the presence of a blonde haired young woman.

"My name is Fay Larchy," she spoke to him in his dream.

Fay Larchy gazed at RB as if she understood who he was under the surface. He recognized the image of a smile on her face in the vision and he felt love emanate from the smile to him. The essence of his being started to glow with warmth.

RB was startled awake by the slapping tail of the Furlucci on the water surface again. After a few moments of increased bodily circulation upon awakening, he looked upstream and started his journey anew again.

On the shore to the right he saw a natural pairing of two Mud Sticker Birds, they had long stick like legs and elongated necks. They were called Mud Sticker's because they often poked their long beaks down into the mud of the river bottom or fields in order to find food. They seemed kind of feminine to him. As he stared at the pair their beaks pointed to one another as if they needed to make a decision and in unison they then turned from RB and walked a few steps away. He thought about the relationship of men and women in his life in terms of equality. The birds; a male and a female, looked about the same size and shape. The only difference he could see was a slight discoloration of their feathers. Somehow as he saw this his thoughts turned to that of the woman from his dream, Fay Larchy and then to Tamarack of the Up Falls river village.

As he cruised further upstream on the left he saw a lonesome looking Brownlop. A Brownlop was a four legged animal similar to a Gruntoe, but with brown fur that absorbed light. They had the ability to run and jump quickly through forested areas. He wondered if she too had a mate as the Mud Sticker did, and if she didn't, how she would survive alone. And if she was alone in nature, for how long she would be?

After he went some further distance his inner thoughts were disrupted by the presence of a white billed Paddlequack bird, they were said to be the most vocal of all water swimming birds. There was a noticeable contrast between the Paddlequacks black feathers and its white bill. He felt a oneness with these beings of nature- they were not afraid of him, nor did he scare them. Even the Paddlequack was in harmony as she stared at him and did not utter a caw or even a cluck.

It was getting to be nightfall and RB's boat ran aground on a sandbar. He then consulted his mapping data only to realize that he had exceeded the distance of Navstream data provided by the Worblers.

He tied his boat off safely at that point on the river and laid down. The woven leather blanket provided to him by the Worblers was warm in the cool open air of the night. Exhausted, he rested and gazed at the stars in the sky. The patterns they provided him with reassured him of his position and orientation relative to home.

He found the pull tab switch on the inside of his jacket that converted the sunlight it captured during the day into heat to keep him warm throughout the night. As he started to warm up he saw that the sixteen spheres had risen from his boat and were now floating in the air above him.

Four of the spheres positioned themselves directly over RB's head in a square pattern. The square of four spheres rotated as if they were a spinning wheel in the sky. They then came to an abrupt stop. The Sphere that was in the direction of RB's home briefly changed color to crimson red.

At this point four more spheres formed another square. This square was smaller than the first. The second square rotated on a plane in the air and superimposed itself within the first square.

Together these two squares rotated as one and again stopped. The Sphere that pointed in the direction of RB's home briefly changed color to neon blue.

The eight remaining spheres then formed an octagon that was smaller than the second square. The octagon of spheres superimposed and aligned itself with the other two spheres that had formed a star.

The star pattern of sixteen spheres then rotated as one and stopped and again the sphere that pointed in the direction of RB's home briefly changed color, this time to green.

He looked at the spheres in the air and watched them as they formed a straight horizontal line. A letter briefly formed in each of the spheres. R B U R M A K E R S S EED. RB looked at the letters that formed and wrote them down on a portable annotation type pad.

The sixteen spheres then lined up in the air above RB in two rows of eight per each row. Then in what looked to be random movements the spheres each systematically moved to locate opposite on a plane that was the shape of a square. Such a square if completely filled with a full array of spheres would have the dimensions of eight spheres by eight spheres. After they switched from one side of the ephemeral square to the other in this way several times they then moved and blinked all over the eight by eight dimensional plane created by their placement in space. The changing patterns of color had some meaning on the unconscious level to RB.

The spheres then formed an exact lifelike image of RB in the sky. Like it was indeed a duplicate of himself floating in the air.

The spheres then all flew close together and formed a unified Glommerate type structure. RB saw a flash of white light form as the spheres disappeared into a white plane of light that faded as it traveled away from its center point in all directions; on this plane.

'***

Meanwhile as the horizon event created by the spheres radiated outward in a pulse, it passed over Helmoot as he rested with Ms. Hillsmith, his healing accelerated and he was healthy again.

'***

With this sense of place RB slept through the night, and did not find noises distant or close much of a bother to him.

When RB walked down to the shoreline to get into his Cauldron Skipper as the sun rose he saw that two long legged Mud Sticker birds were standing by his boat. One of the Mud sticker birds looked into the boat and then at RB. It raised its left knee in the air and the knee jutted forward and pointed at the deck of the boat. To RB it looked like with its next step it wanted to get in his boat.

"Shoo! Shoo!" RB sternly said to the pair of Mud Stickers.

The Mud Stickers did not move, instead the Mud Sticker who was closer to RB pointed its beak in the boat. Almost as if it wanted to say if it could speak, *"I want to get in your boat. I was flying overhead and saw you in that boat. You will take me for a ride."*

RB looked sternly at the Mud Sticker birds, pointed his finger at them and said sternly again, "Shoo! Shoo!" He then waved at the Mud Sticker birds for them to move away from his boat. The pair of Mud Sticker birds did indeed move away from his boat but the skinny long stick legged birds with plump round mid sections and pointy beaks on long necks ducked into the forest and secretly watched RB as he traveled up river. RB did not notice.

He sensed what he would find ahead. He was confident that the river he was on would eventually lead to an interim formation of a lake. And that upon traveling across the lake he would find the mouth of the river and proceed upstream on the river toward home again.

17 SAWMILL MAN

As RB taxied slowly upstream using only solar power based propulsion, he came to a saw mill on the rightward shore. The big paddle wheel of the mill was faithfully turning in the otherwise quiet current.

There was a short T-shaped pier jutting out in the river and it had mooring cleats on it. Past the churning wheel that powered the mill, quarried steps led the way up to a door on the side of the saw mill. A sign on the door read "Sawmill Man's Sawmill. Open"

RB was intrigued by the place and a little blanched from the journey and in need of some human interaction or company. He tied his Skipper securely to the dock in two places and lunged up onto the dock. Somewhat hobble legged from being on the water he climbed the stairs to the mill.

He knocked on the door and there was no answer. So he opened the door, stuck his head in and hollered, "Is anyone here?" His initial view revealed to him a well-lit, open and organized shop. Layers of heavy boards were neatly stacked on shelves that looked capable of holding great weight. The boards were of various types' grain patterns and complementary colors of wood. From the doorway he could see orange grains and whitish colored wood with darkened grain patterns. As he looked at the grain patterns and formations he thought, *"This is the art of God I am looking at."*

His admiration for the place was broken when he saw a stout man approaching from two open doors on the other side of the building. Not wanting to seem like he was up to no good RB said aloud, "Hello" and continued, "I am traveling homeward on the river and decided to stop in and see what you do here, my name is RB."

The two shook hands and the other man said, "I'm Sawmill Man."

"Is that your name or what you do?" RB asked.

"I am called Sawmill Man," he bluntly replied.

RB continued, "The river current took me down and now I am returning to my village far upstream. You have a very nice mill here. I have always been fond of the art of carpentry."

"Would you like me to show you around the place?" Sawmill Man replied.

"Yes," RB replied.

"Let's go inside the shop and I'll show you the workings," Sawmill Man said and led RB further into the building.

"As logs come in they are decked."

"What does that mean?"

"Sorted by species and further by size and further by end use application."

Sawmill Man continued, "We call this machine a Rough although with modernizations it does not make as rough cuts as it initially did. Its head saw is used to cut logs into smaller logs which we call cants and also to then cut into flitches which are unfinished planks. The round blade of the saw is powered by the paddlewheel you saw in the river. The wheel also powers the conveyor belt which pulls the wood along."

"Very interesting," RB replied.

Momentarily RB then thought of how in his spare time he could fashion himself a push pole to use on shoals. He thought of how he could make it out of the yellow wood he'd seen in the shop and two blades cut from one of his old malformed propellers that he kept as spares in his boat.

Sawmill Man continued, "The round blade can be adjusted to different angles."

"This machine over here with the big mouth smoothes the surface of the wood. It either planes or sands depending upon which lever I pull. The edger takes the flitch off the planks and then the ends are trimmed to square. In that building over there dust from the millings is used to dry the wood in a kiln. RB would you mind helping me lift that larger log over there."

"I would be happy to," RB replied.

RB and Sawmill Man, working in unison, hoisted the log onto the mills buckboard feed and Sawmill Man further positioned it.

Sawmill Man looked to RB to see if RB had mutual sense of understanding and then pulled a lever which gradually brought the gear that powered the blade up to speed. He then pulled another and the log was conveyed through the saw.

When the log made its way through Sawmill Man turned off the mill and the two went to look at the result.

"This wood is beautiful, what kind is it?" RB asked.

"It's Yellow Sapscent, it's not as common today and it has a good hardness to it," replied Sawmill Man.

The two slid the bulk of the log back to the other end of the machine and repeated the process.

"***

"That's all we do this way today. We must have cut and stacked eighty board, didn't seem to take long either," Sawmill Man said.

"It did seem to go quickly," RB replied.

"Thank you for helping me today. Would you like to stay on awhile?"

"I think I would like to stay awhile. It looks like there are plenty of things I could learn here," RB answered.

"That would be good as I could use some help for awhile. I expect to see settlers here soon," Sawmill Man said.

"Sawmill Man are you getting hungry?"

"Yes but before I make us something to eat, we need to cut a few pieces into short and precise lengths for a project I am working on. If you would be so kind as to grab two planks from that stack there and bring it to the table of the saw so that we can rough cross cut it to length."

"I certainly would."

RB then watched as Sawmill Man measured two foot sections and marked them off with a writing instrument made of bound and compressed ashes.

"If you would be so kind as to steady the long end of the board while we then, on my command, move it together quickly in unison, in order to keep the board at a right angle to the blade while we cross cut."

"I got it."

RB stood holding the weight of the length of boards near their end while Sawmill Man stood closer to the blade. Sawmill Man fastened a board at a right angle to the pair of boards, he was to cut. This formed a guide as it butted up against the edge of his saw table.

"Okay RB, together, now we cut."

Sawmill Man walked forward while guiding and maintaining control of the boards and RB tried to move just the same as he did so as not to bind the wood to the saw. Two small sections were cut to length and they rested on the top of the saw table, the side opposite the blade from Sawmill Man and RB.

"Okay RB you hold these while I walk around and clear the two cut pieces."

RB held the boards. Sawmill Man and RB repeated the process until all cuts were made.

"Where shall we stack these boards?" RB asked.

"Right inside by the back door," Sawmill Man answered.

RB stacked the boards by the shop door of the saw mill for Sawmill Man.

"Let's have something to eat now. I'll go get some scrap wood for a grilling fire."

"Where do you keep the fire wood?" RB asked.

"Just outside the back door are some scrap pieces that were parsed out as scrap for low grade quality. I'll go get some," Sawmill Man stated.

"I can do it," RB said and made his way to the back of the shop.

"Okay if would you be so kind we need five scrap boards from outside for a bonfire."

RB retrieved five short boards from outside the back door of the saw mill.

18 THE PAINTER

RB awoke before sunrise and looked at his cabin surroundings a little closer. It had the basic amenities of a guest room; a stool in the corner and a painting of a woman on the wall.

RB walked outside. He noticed that Sawmill Man had a light on his living quarters and that his door was open so that he decided to say good morning to him.

RB knocked at the open archway to Sawmill Man's door as he saw that he was busy in his room. He had an easel in front of him and was indeed painting a picture of a woman.

"Good morning Sawmill Man. You are a painter?"

"Well yes I am. I am self taught. At first I just sat in front of my newly made paper and didn't know what to do. I did not want to ruin it. Then I just took the clean brush with no paint on it and started to pretend to paint- without paint. After a while of making empty brush strokes on the paper I decided to see what paint would look like on the paper. So I made some colors up out of everyday things that had such colors and just painted general forms on the canvas in the different colors.

Finally I just started to paint things with the paint and it has worked out quite well for me. I mean that I am pleased with how my paintings turn out."

"She's beautiful."

"What the heck, a guy gets lonely. So I found that I started painting images of women…I really enjoy painting. I once had some strips of wood that I did not know what to do with so I connected four pieces together at the ends and made a rectangular frame out of them. I looked at the rectangular frame and decided that I needed to do something with it, so I figured out a way to make a cloth like paper and attach it to a frame."

"How do you make your cloth like paper?" RB asked.

"Well I will show you," Sawmill Man said as he tidied his painting brush clean with a cloth. "Let's go back to the mill," Sawmill Man said as he led RB to the sawmill. Sawmill Man went to his sawmill accessory shelf and reached up for an attachment.

"This is like the meal grain powder maker but instead of making grain meals it grinds waste products up to make paper. I keep a pile of just such grass, bark and wood wastes out back to use to grind up with this machine to make paper with."

"Let's go get some," Sawmill Man said as he completed attaching his wood grinding flake adapter to his sawmill. Sawmill Man then led RB out back and from a wood box he filled a large basket with this scrap waste. Sawmill Man lifted the basket in front of him and walked back to the mill as RB followed him. Sawmill Man then pulled the gradient lever that powered the mill and the cutting gears of the pulp flake grinder started to turn.

"RB, could you grab that basket; the one sitting on the floor by the wall?"

"I got it," RB said as he got the basket and then placed it under the output shoot of the pulp flake grinder. Sawmill Man then fed the scrap and field type waste into the intake of the machine. First he put in a large strip of tree bark, then some prickly golden grasses and then some small wood strips and lastly he poured some sawdust into the bowl shaped intake of the machine. Pulp flakes and small wood powders filled the basket below the output shoot.

As Sawmill was drawn into the beauty of his work RB thought he heard him whisper with his tongue protruding from between his lips, "Felled woods barks works best...and softly cores trees parts."

When Sawmill Man was done feeding the waste material into the machine and the outflow of it stopped he pulled the gradient power lever off, the machine stopped turning and he said, "Now we need twice as much warm water as we have pulp flakes. I keep a reservoir of water ready for just such purposes. It is very simple in that it is a black basin and the water in it heats up from the sunlight it receives during the day. The water in the river tends to be colder and does not work as well. The process just works better with warm water. It breaks down the pulp flake to pulp quicker." Sawmill Man walked to the side of the mill as RB followed him. He picked up two large buckets, handed one to RB and walked to the basin as RB followed. Sawmill Man turned a valve on the reservoir and the warm water that flowed from the spigot filled his bucket. He turned off the spigot and set his bucket to the side to make room for RB's bucket. RB put his bucket under the spigot and Sawmill Man opened the valve to the spigot tap above it and warm water flowed into the bucket.

Sawmill Man closed the valve and took his bucket to the outdoor work table while RB followed. RB placed his bucket next to Sawmill Mans and followed him back into the mill.

"What parts do we need next," RB asked.

"When I made that first wood frame I attached a cloth to the frame. It would serve as a strainer, whereby the pulp flake and warm water mixture will settle out and the natural fiber type glues in the scrap material will re-solidify and keep the paper together while it dries out," Sawmill Man said as he grabbed the cloth straining frame and a frame that was just a bit larger in size that the straining frame. "This frame is a reservoir frame. It has a box bottom so that I can fill it with water so that the pulp settles out more evenly in the water bath created."

Sawmill Man placed box bottom frame on the outdoor workbench and then placed the straining frame inside it. He then started to ladle pulp flake from the basket into one of the warm buckets of water. As he added the pulp flake he stirred the mixture. He felt with the ladle as he added pulp flake and stirred and when he had discerned that he had a mixture to his choosing he stopped stirring and took the other warm bucket of water and filled his box frame apparatus with it to the level of about his thumb. He then picked up his pulp flake/ water mixture and poured it in the box frame. He used the bottom of his universal ladle to smooth it out to an even layer in the cloth screening frame. When he was done leveling it he said to RB, "When I lift the pulp strainer up you pull the frame off to the side and dump the water. Sawmill Man lifted, RB scuttled the box frame and Sawmill Man carefully set the pulp filled frame back down on the top of the outdoor workbench table. "I will let this dry naturally for some time before I flip it over on a box bottom frame that is just slightly smaller than the opening of this box frame, the paper will dry solid naturally then."

"Well you showed me something neat to do again," RB said to Sawmill Man. The two then sat on stools near the outdoor workbench table and RB asked, "What do you use to make your paints with?"

"Oh, various things. For the golden skin color I use the inside of the coppernicus bulb. For red I use a dried berry extract. For yellow I use a flower pedal. For blue I use a mineral powder. All of these can be mixed with my basic wood oil concoction to make the paint better."

"I was once told that the coppernicus bulb pulls the gold colored metal from the ground that surrounds it and concentrates it in the bulb."

"I believe that is true."

"Have you ever tried mixing your paint powders with a Horloff extract?"

"No I have never tried that, but I believe that might have some validity as a technique," Sawmill Man answered.

19 PENGAVILLY

Sawmill Man and RB started mill work again. It turned out to be a good morning's work with two nice stacks of boards to show for it.

RB stacked the last board on top of the layer and then skewed it slightly left and right to compare it to the one below it.

Sawmill Man was at the well and drinking from a ladle. He scooped a fresh cold ladle of well water and brought it to RB who was standing beside the boards. RB took a drink of the water as Sawmill Man looked at the stack.

"Don't you know… don't you know… that it is impossible for you're sawmill to turn because it is placed at a constant elevation point on the river."

"And yet it is, isn't it."

"Yeah well it shouldn't be."

"What are you going to say next? That it isn't because it shouldn't be?"

"No."

"Well then?"

"Well, can you explain it then?"

"Of course I can." Sawmill Man said and then paused…

"Well, are you going to?"

"Do you want me to?"

"You can start now."

"Just below the paddlewheel is what we call a Hurkle Burkle. You know what a Hurkle Burkle is, don't you?"

"No, I have to admit that I don't."

"A Hurkle Burkle is a hole in the bottom structure where new water comes from; water that did not make its way downstream with the rest."

"Well I do know what one is but I never heard it called that before."

"The water in this one springs up very quickly from the river bottom and I rather ingeniously placed my sawmill here to tap into this motion. I located the paddlewheel just far enough out from shore whereby I can dip my feet in the Hurkle Burkle from time to time."

"You're kidding!"

"I have a pair of polished shell goggles that you can use to swim down and see with."

"No, that's alright."

"RB, I suppose you are going to head upstream soon on your journey back."

"This place is starting to feel like home to me, but home is still home," RB replied.

Sawmill Man stared at the last skewed board on top and said, "Sometimes the exposed layer of grain of wood can be thought of kind of like a slice of life."

"I kind of know what you mean."

"You can see the life cycle through many years by looking at the milled layer."

"It's beautiful, the natural patterns that form."

"Sometimes it doesn't seem fair that we use it for our purposes."

"It didn't speak up when we milled it."

"Maybe it did but we didn't hear it," Sawmill said jokingly and they both laughed.

"Have you always lived here?" RB asked.

"No. Before I came here I lived for awhile at a place called Pengavilly."

"I want to tell you about a place upstream from here, you might encounter it on your trip home. But you don't want to go there or hear about it," Sawmill said and there was a long pause that was broken when RB asked,

"What kind of place?...Why not?"

"As I said the place is called Pengavilly," Sawmill Man said sternly and paused before speaking again.

"The name sounds evil," RB commented.

Sawmill Man looked RB solemnly in the eyes and said, "It was, and the people there were different."

"How so?"

"Their eyes will not be their own. You can tell of this because the mannerisms of the men were not of men, but of women, and the mannerisms of the women were not of the women but more or less of the men. You know it is a long story from a long time ago and I suppose we have time so I'll tell it to you. One day I set out on my own looking for a better life. As you know I have many woodworking skills. I had built myself a large wooden raft like boat and took my belongings and headed downstream looking for a place with lots of people to settle in. I thought I might find a place to trade or a nice community to settle in. I got pretty far downstream and then I saw the figures of a pair of beautiful women, in a carved out boat, push poling their way into a side channel, some distance away. I hollered 'Hello,' but they didn't hear me so I decided to follow them to see where there might be a settlement. Up their river shoot a way's, a sign read Pengavilly."

"I have never heard of it before," said RB.

"It was an okay place to settle. I built a small house on the outskirts and the people seemed decent. But gradually it got kind of strange to live there. One family nearby had three sons; the oldest named Klatch. The two youngest named Scratch and Patch were exactly the same- identical in age and looks. They would hide and wait for their older brother to come outside. He was about four or five complete season sets older than them. They would then ambush him, tackle and bully. At first I thought it was funny, those little guys all over him, but after awhile it started to tear at my heart."

"Didn't his parents do anything to stop it?" RB asked.

"No they were of the boy's will be boy's philosophy."

"One day I got tired of being distracted by this and I yelled at them. I said, 'You hate yourself and the image of yourself more than anyone or anything else. You know already what you will never be and you know what you can never be. Now leave your older brother alone.'"

"Why'd you say it like that?"

"I don't know the words just came to me at the time."

"Well, what happened next?"

"Why then their mother came to talk to me about them. Now, all the women there were different. No matter what they did they always walked kind of alluring. It was almost as if their walk was saying to me, "You can't spank me." It seemed like opportunistically they would also dance around when I was doing something, kind of like showing me what they could do or hey look at me. When I tried to talk to them, for courting though, I had very little luck. Aside from all their pretense a relationship with one never would seem to pan out."

"Were the men sound? What were they like?" RB asked.

"Well the women and for that matter the village was governed by the men and they were short and walked like plump fannied birds with stick legs."

"You mean like Mud Sticker Birds?"

Sawmill Man thought a second and said, "Well yeah. As they walked by they'd often glance back with longing eyes to see if I desired them, and I don't really want to say this but it is what I believe, as women. They weren't like men we might know of, it was more like they were possessed by the dark natured women."

"Were they all like that?"

"No. Some of their women were born kind of ugly or crotchety like. They were kept in a small village separate from the rest, governed by a small group of men without ambitions', backbone or stance."

"You're speculating, Sawmill Man," RB said with a smile.

"No, I once asked a village elder, 'Why do they keep those women up there?' He replied, 'The only way they could stand her was if she was bothering somebody else. She was born sore-like. And acted like she had spent too much time on the Horloff churn or resented she had to use one at all. They didn't know what to do with those queer sons either, so they put them with them. Figuring there's a little strength in them to take care of them. Maybe they'd be good for each other. Another young man was raised to be so jealous of others that he became physically ill. White phlegm was even seen dripping from his mouth from the illness. They started to call him, 'The it's still smiling from the last time it bit you!' as there was something evil and Surpedo like about him. They put him up there too. ' Anyhow I would look outside often before going out to do some work and nobody would be outside, but the moment I went outside they would mostly all have to go outside also, and cause all kinds of commotion and distraction."

"Really?"

"Yes. It seems they liked to watch me work. Their skills were crude and primitive, the way they fashioned things, miss-fitted workings. And whatever clothes I would decide to wear that day they would all come out wearing ones of theirs that looked the same as mine."

"Like they started to admire you?"

"Well yes, but it was different or worse than that. Whenever I would do something the men would watch and try to do the same work. When they got good they would try and best me. Then they would pretend it was them who all along thought of the stuff I was doing. Then out of frustration I would do something new and they all had to do that too."

He continued, "The sons seemed to be born hating their fathers. I think out of the fathers' frustrations, they would tell the sons that their father was someone else other than them and that is who they ended up bothering instead. It was as if they denied their responsibility as a father."

"I'm starting to get a picture of this. They thought of you as a father," RB said.

"Well you might look at it that way, but it was worse. When the sons and fathers seemed to learn something from me it was if they didn't feel like they really knew it until I didn't know it anymore."

"What are you talking about?" asked RB.

"Whenever I would do my work, they would bother me and distract me until things that were easy and common for me became hard to do. I could tell that after awhile of this I would lose my capability altogether and become dependent on them and whatever treatment or devises they had for me. Because they were watching me so often, one time I tried to give them advice on their makings and it was like, if there are less people to tell or know their work is bad, it means their workings are actually better. So eventually I decided to leave. Then the night before I had planned to leave there was a celebration in the commons. They threw some weird leaves in the fire. I was captivated by its smell. After I smelled it the women were asking me for maker's seed. 'Give us maker's seed!' they said to me. They liked that maker seed whatever it was and then they would saunter away to their dwellings, where their men would greet them and act all tough like I couldn't have a woman. Like they were too good for me or better than me. Then another would come by and say, 'Give me maker's seed.' And before I could speak she was gone.

Pretty soon I was dizzy and some of the men started acting affectionate to me. One of them had mean little beady eyes like something you'd see staring at you at the edge of a clearing where you have a camp fire lit. He got red in the face when I said, "I have nothing for you." He went away and I snuck off and ran fast and got away. From there on after I slept scared in my dwelling.

After that day they treated me differently. They seemed more like a gang of men and women than a friendly community. The men would sometimes stare at me like I was some kind of a ghost. The women desperately acting like they wanted my affection, even angry like. But when I talked to them, I couldn't form a relationship.

I wasn't able to leave right away after that.

The women always seemed interested but then never were. When I talked to them I could not retain my soul. It led me to helplessness. They were odd people, seemingly not brought up as I traditionally know people to be. The women were beautiful, but they were emotionally abused by the males in the household until they did their bidding or evil for them. It changed them to something of a vicious and spiteful nature.

It was as if my spirit was becoming less and less for me and more and more for them. They seemed to be able to track my doings as if part of my spirit. And acted as if my spirit was theirs and not mine."

Sawmill Man paused in sad reflection and then continued, "Who is it that thinks that everything that isn't theirs actually belongs to them anyway?"

RB couldn't answer.

"Some of the men were more evil and the women partnered with them because they had more belongings. However, once together the women weren't treated well by the men. The men lost ambition and the women were forced to do evil to attain and keep wealth, because the husbands, while being abusive, were also worthless and dependent.

After the ceremony night with the leaves in the fire I was in a daze.

The men seemed to be as easily influenced or possessed by one woman as the next. And I could see that they were often unfaithful to each other. When they were possessed their eyes were not their own. I could also tell of this because their mannerisms would no longer be of men but of woman. They will be curtsy like and often haunch on all fours whenever ostensibly possible. Sometimes the strongest of their men walked like they were wearing skirts, but they weren't.

One time a beautiful woman with a larger belly walked by me. As she passed by she said, 'I've got one of you in here.' The women seemed to like me or want to possess me. Sometimes they seemed like they felt scorned even though they weren't. The men, red faced, would often haunt me, saying vile words. They went to great lengths of fury to try and break my spirit, as if to prove they were better. I never felt I was better but I know I had more skill to begin with."

RB listened intently to Sawmill Man.

"Once the women would catch sight of someone as good looking and strong as you, the process would be unstoppable. If the women like you, they try and possess you. And the men will haunt you. If you went there you would be in trouble. And you will be going in that general direction to get home."

"Well, what happened?" RB asked.

"Well, once you go there it is very hard to leave. One day I was doing some work and some of the older women came by. When they got older they didn't look so beautiful anymore. One hag in the group said, 'Who knows something bouts him makes him cry?'…'Make room for me I want to look at him,' said another. I looked the other way to ignore them and there I saw a younger woman was naked and washing herself outside- while one poses a distraction the other looks compromising."

A hag looked at me furiously and said, 'Don't you look at her, ever!'

'I haven't done anything wrong here,' I said. They spewed a few more insults at me, and my face started to weaken and maybe I started to cry. When they made me feel miserable about myself they felt a lot better about themselves. They seemed to glow after this. It was as if when they were to see you the least bit relaxed or happy their self delusions of being you or better than you started to fade rapidly and then they begin to cry. They will spew out insults, and as you start to feel miserable they start to feel better about themselves."

They once said, "Oh why we makes him cry; now I cries too."

"Well, what happened next?" RB asked.

"Well, I noticed that if I were to go for walks and get a little away from them, I started to feel more like myself. My memory and my knowledge of skills started to return. After awhile of this they seemed to follow me wherever I went though, to try to diminish this. Let's go for a little walk," Sawmill Man concluded.

Seeing that Sawmill Man was uptight from the story he told, RB started to tell a story he knew to reset their mood and calm his new friend.

"My father told me a story of those Crockus Birds, floating in the river there...before he went missing," RB said as he waved his hand to the birds in the river while they walked the path along shore.

"I have heard some stories of Crockus Birds," Sawmill Man said.

"One good story deserves another," RB replied.

"It sure does."

"My memory of the names in the story is not so good, but once upon a time, one Crockus bird had a different pattern of feathers on its back, or crest is maybe the word. The other Crockus's outcast him, made him a pariah. As an outcast he enjoyed his time by himself and seemed to thrive. So the others started to spy on him, as he went to where he pecked for food here and there. One day the Crockus realized just this and the others realized he realized this and they attacked him and pecked at his feathers. And he lost some feathers. So he went further away, but the group of Crockus birds became uneasy and enraged at not knowing what he was up to. Alone and away, the outcast Crockus bird reflected upon events and somehow became stronger.

The group of Crockus birds always followed the mother in a row when they were young. They were all raised, or imprinted by, or imprinted with her temperament. A very few of the male birds, had a male demeanor like his, because they were born and raised to mock him, the stronger outcast. By fighting him, the pariah, who was once one of them, the others gained status in the group or pecking order."

RB reflected to himself out loud in epiphany, "Maybe my father was meaning to speak of men and not birds? Anyhow, the pariah would never find a mate and they all died as they were fixated on the pariah and could think of nothing else with regards to or in ignorance of their greater good. Well, that is the gist of the story, what I sifted from it logically and reworded now to suit myself."

Sawmill Man chimed in, "To teach false reasoning for things repeats failure, faster than not teaching at all. One day I did come out of my dwelling mad and yelled at those of Pengavilly. I had written it all down so I could say it all good without losing my place as to what I'd say and look foolish instead, but this is the gist."

"You are cowardly, queer and weak!

How can your woman stand you? They make all the earns and do all the work for you.

You will never have a soul!

You are not men; you are the antithesis of men! People raised like you can never lead; they will only be followers, and disgruntled ones at that!

Your women pity you and your children and the world gives you a favor by giving you a head start!

Your intelligence stolen is never greater than from whom you stole it!

You women are as cowardly and run when talked to by the ones they desire! They seek to have him in another way! To make their men like him! And in the process destroy him! You clean your conscience of guilt and responsibility by accusing someone else of something you do!"

And my face was filled with anger and rage as I yelled, "You can never be me, and this is the source of your self hatred, this conflict created and maintained by you! This jealous idolatry! You expect good service while you cannot provide it! It is not in your nature! You could not take criticism regarding food that you dish out!"

From what I know about them: Your energy state of consciousness is then shared by them; after all in this fugue state of being, you won't have your own, because they have it. They won't share it with you; they will do everything in their power to prevent you from thinking.

They are weak minded and not strong enough even to handle your pity of them.

Ask them the simplest question and they have dumbfounded looks like you are trying to put them to an intelligence test and none of their answers would be smart ones, so they don't answer.

I told the Pengavillians all this too, 'You will never be able to think for yourself. You never share willingly. You have been spoon fed plenty. You will want everything spoon fed to you. You don't even remember the questions I ask you.' Standing up for myself did not seem to make a difference regarding their attitudes towards me."

"What happened next?"

Sawmill Man continued, "After that, at night I could hear howls in the woods and about the place. Sounded like a growling beast hiding and waiting to pounce on me and render with claws. Made one scared to leave and the people hadn't changed. But by being away from them for even the slightest moment my strength came back very quickly.

One day I walked a short distance from the village and pretended to be doing something good. I cautioned away everyone that came near. Then I dug up some roots for dinner. Come to think of it I did hit some rocks with the shovel… they were more like large flat stones. I brushed them off some and they had some letters and words chiseled into them. But I didn't pay much more attention to it, than that, because I was looking to leave fast. Later in the day after dinner I went to go to relieve myself downstream, as I always did.

As I expected, all the men then ran to where I had been working to see what I had been doing. At which point I ducked behind some trees and just started running fast and silently. With none of my possessions I ran and ran. When I got far away I found a river and jumped in to cool off. I started to drift and drift, floating face up with the current and after awhile I drifted near shore here, stood up in the shallows and this is my home."

"That is some story," RB finally said.

"It is true I tell you, and you want to avoid it," Sawmill Man looked RB in the eye knowing he was a good man, and RB looked Sawmill Man in the eye with a sense of belief and understanding.

"They… those women… they sound like Medika and Shurlene," RB caught himself thinking aloud.

"They are?"

"Two women that ran me over the falls."

"You let two women run you over a falls?"

"Yeah, and that seems like them."

Sawmill Man blinked, nodded and blinked his eye's solemnly.

"Why were they evil? I keep asking myself," RB said.

"Because no one could stop them from being so. To teach them differently. They never were made to learn the consequences of their actions, and continued to do bad things."

"Like a game of enjoyment."

"Since I have been here I have always thought this would be a good place to start a village," Sawmill Man said.

"From what I have seen I agree with you."

20 IT WALKS THE PLANK

The two ate lunch with their feet dipped in the warm Hurkle Burkle water. And as the afternoon progressed the mood turned rather jovial.

"How many boards is a board foot?" RB asked Sawmill Man.

"A foot is twelve twelve's," Sawmill Man replied.

"My foot isn't."

"Well, how many boards are there in your foot?"

"There are no boards in my foot," RB replied.

"Well how many boards are there in a bored foot?"

"My foot isn't bored."

"No I mean like wood."

"Bored like wood? You mean drilled a hole in wood?"

"No I mean boards like planks."

"So how many planks in a board foot?"

"How long is the plank?"

"You mean the board?"

"Yes."

"Well that's what I'm asking you, how many boards in a linear board foot?"

"Linear means line."

"Well that would be a narrow board."

"I thought it was a plank?"

"No it's a board."

"There is none. It's a board."

"What's it aboard a ship?"

"Well sometimes they are."

"You mean when they ask you to walk one like from the legends of the privateers- walk the plank?"

"Don't you mean board?"

"No you said that. Plank!"

"Like on a ship, or deck of a ship?"

"Yes that's what you said."

"Well then how many of those are there in a board foot?"

"Well how wide is the foot?"

"That depends on how big it is."

"You mean as in feet?"

"Yes."

"We can tell by how big a shoe you wear."

"What the hell are you talking about?"

"What you said."

"No I was asking about how many boards in a board foot."

"Yes, a linear board foot."

"A foot is twelve twelve's a foot."

"So how many of your boards can you fit in twelve twelve's."

"That depends on how wide the boards are."

"Isn't that what I'm asking you?"

"What exactly are you asking me?"

"Look if the directions say I need so many board feet, how much is… how many do I need?"

"Well then you follow the directions."

"But I don't know how many board feet are in them."

"It depends on how wide the boards are."

"How wide are the boards?"

"It's not in the instructions."

"Then they can be any width?"

"How do I know then?"

"You don't."

"What do you mean I don't. You mean I don't know?"

"Yes, you figure that out later."

"How can I plan for it then? In order to plan for something you have to figure it out first."

"No that's not what I meant."

"Well that's what you said."

"Yes but not what I mean."

"Well why did you say it?"

"I thought you would understand."

"How can I understand if it's not what you meant, what you said?"

"Well then you have to ask."

"Well that's what I'm doing. How many boards in a board foot?"

"How wide is the board?"

"Well it appears you have different widths for sale. So I am asking you."

"Well we need to think in square feet."

"You don't sell any boards in square feet."

"Yes I do."

"I don't see any square foot boards."

"That's all there is."

"A foot is twelve twelve's so a square foot would be, like this."

"Did you say twelve elf vests?"

"No twelve twelve's," Sawmill Man looked at RB to make sure he understood, "A foot is twelve twelve's so a square foot would be, like this," Sawmill Man gestured with his hands to form a square of twelve twelve's in size.

RB gestured his hands to form a square and said, "I don't see any of those around."

"I'm looking at one right now."

"No I don't mean a viewing box, a square foot. A board twelve twelve's by twelve twelve's."

"Why would you want to buy one of those?"

"I don't!"

"Well that's what you asked for."

"No I didn't, I asked how many boards are in a board foot."

"What's the foot a board?"

"No. Feet aren't boards."

"Feet aren't aboards a what?"

"Feet aren't made of boards."

"A privateer's was."

"No a privateer's was a peg, not a foot."

"You mean his leg."

"Yes."

"He didn't have a leg, he had a peg."

"How do you know he had a peg?"

"Well I was assuming he lost his leg."

"Why would you assume that?"

"Because if a privateer had a foot made of wood, it would mean he had a peg leg, not a foot and peg legs were made of wood."

"Why would you assume a privateer's had a peg leg?"

"Because you suggested it."

"I never suggested you had a peg leg."

"I don't have a peg leg. Why did you suggest it?"

"I didn't suggest it you did."

"I wouldn't have suggested that I have a peg leg."

"But that's what you said."

"No I never said that you had a peg leg either."

"Yes you did."

"And you don't?"

"Of course I don't, because I'm not a privateer. But if I was a privateer and didn't have a leg I would probably have a peg leg."

"And you don't because you are not a privateer?"

"No because I don't have one."

"And you don't mean you have to be a privateer to have one."

"No you have to lose your leg to have it replaced by a board, I mean a peg."

"And you haven't lost your peg?"

"No I never had one."

"You've got two feet?"

"Yes I have two feet!"

"Are they bored feet?"

"No they are not bored feet! I told you I don't have board feet!"

"Well then you go walk on your feet not of boards, that can walk on boards, and find me this board in your storefront!"

"What do you mean this board?"

"I need some thin strips of boards to make a push pole staff," RB said.

"Oh, you can find some of those stacked up behind the main stack."

As RB walked to the stack he thought of how he got along with his friend Old Josey back home and how he and Tamarack seemed to agree with each other.

21 RB'S POLE STAFF

RB had found some thin strips of wood about half the thickness of his small finger by half the length of his index finger. They were of different colors dark and light. Sawmill Man, seeing RB looking fondly at them, explained the types of wood to him.

"The dark wood is Braccus. Braccus is a hard wood. It grows near the shore and is dense like a metal. It is often used as ballast. The white colored wood is called Waxnord and is nearly unbreakable."

"I thought these two would go well together," RB said.

"What do you mean, go good together?" Sawmill Man asked.

"I plan on binding them together to make a push pole staff. Mine was lost. The different colored woods would contrast each other in the staff. What do you want for them?"

"The help you gave with the boards is pay enough. But I am curious to how you make your push pole staff. And must watch how you do it. Why do you not just make one from one larger single piece? Here I'll show you the walking staff that I made."

"The way I make one is stronger," RB said before Sawmill Man returned with his walking staff.

Sawmill Man handed the staff to RB and said, "It is almost perfectly rounded from end to end."

RB held the walking staff and examined it. He tested it for balance and said, "Very nice workmanship."

RB handed the pole to Sawmill Man who stood with it proudly, as if he was about to go walking with it, as he watched RB work some more.

RB took the wood strips to the work bench and clamped one to the top. He then took his shivum shaver and shaved off a thin slice of wood from the end of one.

"May I borrow your ash bound writing instrument?" RB asked.

"Sure. It's called an ABW for short," Sawmill Man answered and handed RB his ABW.

RB took the thin strip he had shaven off and marked off the length of the short side of it on a flat scrap piece of wood. Then RB turned the long side to this marking and marked the long side with the ABW to the same length as the short side. He then took the straight edge of one of his wood strips and used it to draw a straight line from edge to edge where he had made his mark on the long side. Effectively RB had marked off a square. Then RB took his straight edge wood strip and marked off from one corner of the square to the other with the ABW. Carefully he placed the straight edge of his wood strip to bisect the angle that he created from one corner to the other. So in effect he had half of the angle created by divided the angle from half a square in two.

"Can I borrow a wood knife?" RB asked.

"Sure I keep it right here," Sawmill Man grabbed it and handed it to RB.

RB took the wood knife, felt of the blade and determined that it was sharp enough. RB used it to cut on his ABW markings for his small angle. He held it up in front of him to show Sawmill Man and said, "This will be my template angle."

"Okay, I think I know where you are going. I am watching," Sawmill Man said not wanting to disturb the spirit of RB's work.

RB took his template angle chip and held it to the end of a wood strip, and used the ABW to mark the angle along the edge at the end. Using the ABW he marked the other side of that edge in a corresponding manner. RB parried the strip so the other end of it was in front of him and marked it in the same manner.

"These will serve as guides to how I will remove wood to form a point. When I am done, as you can see the profile of this strip will look like a box that somebody stood on and then started to uniformly collapse to one side before they jumped off," RB explained while showing Sawmill Man the marked ends of the wood strip.

RB then marked the ends of every strip in the same manner. He clamped one to the work bench top with the end hanging off the edge of the work bench. Carefully on the end of the strip he carved a sloping point that corresponded with the ABW mark. Effectively forming a wedge, like something you might use to chisel with. On the opposite end of the piece, the length of which was a third of his height he did the same, but with the chisel like point end facing the other direction. RB repeated the process and carved the same points on every strip of wood.

"Okay now that that part is done I need to go into the forest to get the ingredients to my binder formula. You want to come with?"

"Absolutely, I am quite intrigued by what you are doing," Sawmill Man answered.

They then went walking in the forest and RB found an abandoned Warpesto insect nest in a tree and broke off the branch it was connected to. He placed this pod in his satchel."

"Do you know where there is a Burlett Tree growing nearby?" RB asked.

"Burlett, you said, I think that I have heard it called that, you mean the one that exudes sap?"

"Yes."

"There is one this way," Sawmill Man said as he motioned and led RB through the woods.

As they walked through the woods RB thought of how some people's personalities, from recent memory, were what he could think of as sappy. They kind of stick on you and cause a mess that is hard to clean off. *"They make you sappy too,"* he thought.

RB saw the water's edge approaching as Sawmill Man pointed to a tree and said, "There's one."

"That's the one," RB said thankfully.

RB looked at the long flat and round leaves on the tree and pruned one off with his river knife. He then scraped some sap off the outside of its bark with the back of his knifes blade and wiped it onto the Burlett leaf. He rolled up the leaf, bound it with its stem and placed it in his satchel.

"The last part that I need comes from the river," RB said and led the way to near the water's edge. When RB got fifteen paces from the water's edge he stopped and looked carefully at the river.

"Can I borrow your walking staff?" RB whispered to Sawmill Man.

Sawmill Man understood the whisper meant to be quiet and whispered back, "Yes," and handed RB his staff.

RB had intentionally stopped next to a Hairshoe plant at his side. Carefully RB cut the longest strand from the Hairshoe plant, which was to the right of where they were crouching, and placed it on the ground by his side. He then cut some more Hairshoe strands. He chose one of those and cut a small length from it. This, he placed by the long strand on the ground and the other strands he placed in his satchel. There was a small hole in the blade of RB's river knife near the tip. RB took a long strand of the Hairshoe plant and as he held the handle of his river knife alongside the end of Sawmill Man's walking staff, he wound the strand around both of them and then through the loop he created. He wound around again and then through his the new loop again and pulled tight. He continued to wind in this manner until he reached the end of his knifes handle and then through several loops and ties he was done and the spear was formed. RB picked the short strand, that he had cut, up from the ground and threaded it through the end hole in his knifes blade, that was now a spear point with a barb.

RB looked at Sawmill Man intently. There was a large rock to their left. RB quietly pried it loose from the ground and handed it to Sawmill Man. When Sawmill Man had it in the palm of his hand RB grabbed Sawmill Man's hand with rock in it and strongly moved it up ever so slightly and then downward. This was RB's way to quietly signal to Sawmill Man, *"Beat the fish when I bring it to shore."* He whispered to Sawmill Man, "Wait here until I throw the spear."

RB started to crawl on hands and knees to the river, with his eye's keenly searching below the surface. When he got close to the water he charged upright with his legs and lunged forward with the spear. His body arched to the right and then downward as the spear left the end of his fingertips. The spear broke the water's surface and stuck into the back of a Carpetti fish just behind its head. The portion of the spear seen above the waterline started to sway left and right as the pierced Carpetti started to swim away. RB had two more steps before he was in the water. He ran quickly and leapt upward. With outreached arms he dove for the spear. Just before he reached the water's surface, as he flew, he caught the spear with his hands. He drove the spear further into the Carpetti fish. RB, the spear and the Carpetti fish were driven under the water's surface by the force of RB's diving thrust.

Sawmill Man with rock in hand was at the water's edge when RB came to the surface with fish on spear and flung it high. It arced through the air and landed onto shore. RB swam to where he could stand up and watched as Sawmill Man chased after the fish on spear. Sawmill Man scrambled about as best as he could after the floppy fish and pounced on it. The fish flopped out of Sawmill Man's grasp and he stood back up and took two scurried steps after it and pounced with his hands grabbing for it again. The slippery fish escaped his grasp again and flopped closer to the river's edge. In a last will of renewed youthful effort Sawmill Man finally was able to catch it fast to the ground and bludgeon it with a rock until it moved no more.

"What you laughing at?" Sawmill Man said to RB.

"You're pretty swift for an old hermit."

"A hermit you say! I ought to smack you with her," Sawmill said as he held the fish up by its tail with both his hands and smiled.

"You bashed its head in a little too good."

"Haven't eaten Carpetti fish in awhile, wasn't about to let it get back in the river."

RB stood by Sawmill Man who was panting from unaccustomed exertion. When Sawmill Man's full wind started to return to him RB shook his hand and said, "I didn't know if you still had it in you or not."

Sawmill Man looked peeved at the suggestion and said with a temperamental gruff tone, "Of course I do. Live out alone you can take care of yourself."

RB smiled and found the spear, which had separated from the fish in flight, and unwound his river knife from it. He handed the walking staff to Sawmill Man in no worse shape and sat by the fish on the thick sun browned grass. Carefully he cut open the belly of the fish with his knife; there was a jelly like layer that surrounded its stomach lining and its intestinal cavity. That was the part he was looking for. RB threaded a strand of Hairshoe plant through the gills and mouth of the fish and tied it off. The two fish hunters then walked silently back to the sawmill.

'***

RB saw that Sawmill Man had been watching him intently as he had gathered items for his pole staff and asked him, "Can I borrow a pot?"

"I can't wait to see what you will do next," Sawmill Man said as he quickly went to get RB a pot. As he returned with the pot he said, "Just pretend that I am not watching, I would hate to interrupt the flow of what you are doing and I am learning."

In the pot RB portioned out a measured part of the Warpesto nest and took a rounded stone and worked it into pumice. Then he added a few dab's of the Burlett sap and mixed the powder and sap until it was the same consistency. To that he squeezed in some of the lining from the Carpetti fish and stirred, he checked the consistency of his mixture and squeezed in a little more Carpetti jelly in and then stirred more vigorously.

He then took some of the shorter fibers from a Hairshoe plant and bound them to the end of a short stick with some more Hairshoe strands; in much the same manner as he bound the knife to walking staff. He dipped his new Hairshoe stick brush in the mixture and brushed his fashioned strips of wood with it.

"RB don't you know what the Quilspar plant is good for?"

"Of course I do."

"Well then why aren't you using it?"

"I need the sensation of heavy duty this has."

Once he had two pieces of wood brushed on one side he held them together. They were not exactly the same length. So he was able to form layers that overlapped where the ends met to create stronger length. The chisel shaped ends that he had made earlier fit together snuggly, one after the other. Once he had the rough formation of his staff together in this manner he took some strands of the Hairshoe plant and formed a knotted loop in the ends. He bent the outside of the loop back around itself on both sides and then formed a loop in the length near the end of that loop and stuck it through it. Through that newly formed loop he ran the other end of the strand. He lengthened the strands by tying further strands to the unknotted ends. When he had formed nine of these he placed them around the staff and cinched them up tight. The pieces adjoined together uniformly. He set the staff on a flat and level surface where it would not be disturbed while his nature-made glue dried, and then washed his hands in the river.

"Where did you learn that?" Sawmill Man asked.

"My father taught me."

The next day he picked it up to inspect it. His formula had dried solid and the staff would need a little shaping and finishing work. He took his Shivum Shaver, essentially a blade with two handles on it, and scraped off the glue and a little of the wood. He kept shaving until the end profile formed a square with rounded corners. He then held it in his hands and checked it for weight and balance. He tried to bend it and it would not bend, so he admired his craftsmanship, five layers of wood seamed together with sloping angle joints in the laminate.

The different types of wood contrasted not only in color but also in hardness and other chosen qualities and that made a unified form that gave his staff incredible strength. It was longer than he was tall, and would make a good push pole.

Firmly he grabbed hold of it real tight with both hands, and turned it against the calluses at the base of his fingers on his palms. It made a low growling noise as he turned one hand against the other, the rounded corners vibrated with friction against his grip. He then looked in a storage compartment of his boat for a spare propeller. He knew how to make a push pole head from an old propeller. To his benefit he found a push pole head that he had made long ago and it fit perfectly on his staff.

Sawmill Man had watched him and knew that RB had his staff and was ready to resume his journey home.

"We will have the Carpetti fish for lunch. I have not eaten one in a long time. I know just how to prepare it."

"That sounds good."

"You sure did a nice job making that push pole."

"Thank you, I take pride in a job well done."

'***

Sawmill Man filleted the skin off the Carpetti and then cut four long bone free strips of fish meat from the back of the Carpetti. He set them in a bowl on the counter. He then took his fillet knife and cut through the spin of the Carpetti and made a small steak meat from it. He set the small fish stake meat on a grate where it could drip dry in the sun while he finished filleting the Carpetti into more small steak meats. He went to a shelf in his kitchen and got a jar of white mineral curing salts form it. He had the jar of prepared mineral salts on hand at kept it to his kitchen stock by digging some up from the base of a natural rock formation a quarter of a day's daylight walk away. He prepared the larger bowl with the white mineral curing salts and placed it on his work bench made as kitchen counter. When the fish meats had lost their surface moisture he placed them in the mineral curing salts and tossed them around so that all the small fish meats were covered.

"Let's cook the fish RB. We need one cupping pod from a yellow milk blossom plant," Sawmill Man said.

"I did indeed see one on our walk home. I will go and get it."

As RB went to get the Yellow Milk Blossom plant Sawmill Man got a Jar down from his counter that read Special Spice Mixture for Fish. He sprinkled some in a bowl. He took one half of a bottle labeled Denatured Wood Drink Concoction and poured it in the bowl he put the spice in. Attentively he gave the bowl a stir and then he placed his four fish strips in the bowl.

RB returned with the Yellow Milk Blossom plant and handed it to Sawmill Man. Sawmill Man cut off the pointed crown of the Yellow Milk Blossom plant and squeezed the yellow milk from the blossom into the bowl with the four strips of fish in it. He washed his hands in a clean bucket of fetched water, dried them off and proceeded to toss the fish strips around some more in the bowl of Yellow Milk Blossom, Denatured Wood Drink and spice. He set a plate next to the bowl and then went to look at his kitchen shelf. There were no more powdered grains.

"I have no more grains on my shelf, we will have to pick some," Sawmill Man said.

"Well then let's go get some," RB said.

Sawmill Man and RB walked out into the forest, down the shoreline and inland where they found a small plain with grains growing on it.

"How much do we need to pick?" RB asked.

"You pick enough to hold under the side of your arm while you walk and I will do the same."

Sawmill Man and RB cut and picked the long grain stems. When they each had an armful, Sawmill Man said, "That's enough," and they walked back to the sawmill.

"How do you grind yours into grain powder," asked RB.

"I thought you might ask. I will show you. Follow me," Sawmill Man walked into the part of the sawmill that had the water powered saw in it.

"I have this attachment that I use to do it for me. It fits securely on the side of the power gear to my sawmill. You see I have a designed an accessory attachment fixture fitting to the center of the gear where I can add attachments such as this meal grain grinder." Sawmill Man affixed the grinder attachment to the water powered gear fitting and secured to a fitting that was located separate from the power adapter. Sawmill Man then pulled the gradient drive lever of that put the sawmill blade into action and RB saw the gears of the grain meal grinder had started to turn and weave with together. Sawmill Man placed a bucket under the shoot of the meal grain grinder attachment and then fed a small handful of the grains they had cut earlier into the mouth of the grinder. The golden brown grain grasses were pulled into the grain grinder and small golden and white power wafted into the air from seams of the mechanical device. Before the dry grasses had been fully sucked into the workings of the machine the same golden and white powder slid down the chute of the grinder mill attachment and into the bucket.

"Could you hold the bucket closer to the shoot while I feed the rest of the cut grasses into the machine?"

"I certainly can," RB said as he placed his cut grains on the saw table and held the bucket closer to the chute. When the bucket was close to fill Sawmill Man saw that more than half the grasses were ground and stopped feeding the machine and got another clean empty bucket and placed it under the chute.

The two had two buckets of powdered golden and white grains. Sawmill Man carried one back into the kitchen while RB carried the other. In the kitchen Sawmill Man scooped up a full ladle worth of the powder grains from the bucket and placed the grain powder in a separate bowl. He then took the four fish strips and rolled them in the powder grain of the bowl.

"You have put a nice looking coating on those," RB said.

"It is good to think of new ways to cook food," said Sawmill Man.

The two then went to the cooking fire outside. Sawmill Man placed a grate over the fire and then took the four strips from his bowl and placed them on the grate to cook.

"You can tell they are done when they are golden brown and don't steam anymore…from them," Sawmill Man said as he removed the strips from the grate after they were done.

"Let's eat," he then said.

Sawmill Man then went to the shelf and grabbed an attachment that he then used to mix his drink and also put bubbles in it.

"Would you like to try some of my wood formula drink?" Sawmill Man asked as they were eating the Carpetti.

"Oh, I might try a drop," answered RB.

Sawmill Man poured a little from a jug into RB's cup and RB tried it.

"Tastes kind of like sweet root cider. I was concerned you were going to pour me some of that fuel stuff."

"Oh no. I don't make or drink that. Seen too many people go pale and die from the nature of that."

"Me too."

That night RB was sound asleep, in the lodge for guests that Sawmill Man had built, when he felt all the muscles in his body tense. Without seemingly any control, but more based on instinct, he reflexively grabbed his staff and rose to his feet. He started a powerful swing of his staff to the left. As he bore more force to his staff in those split moments, he turned his head to the left to gain aim and an understanding of the danger present. There he saw a short man formed of glowing red angry colored scheme. The face bore the expression of a cold hearted killer, absent of any regard for fellow being.

The creature had a staff and was lancing it toward RB. RB's gaze seemed to stop the movement of the demon. As the demon slowed, RB's staff bludgeoned through him and destroyed him. Remnants of him evaporated into thin air as he was shattered and destroyed.

RB caught his breath as he watched its ephemeral disappearance and thought to himself, *"Could that have been some aftereffect of Sawmill Man's wood formula drink or was the demon real?"* He went right back to sleep. He got up early that morning and met Sawmill Man outside. Sawmill Man was dressed in his best yellow rain coat and hat.

"I've got my things packed and I am going to be headed upstream now Sawmill Man."

"You made for good company RB and it was good having you work alongside me."

"It was good to work alongside you too Sawmill Man. You were quite hospitable."

"I don't expect I will see you again but if you came back this way you are welcome here."

"If you travel upstream you're welcome too." RB and Sawmill Man shook hands.

When RB was out of sight on the river Sawmill Man started to cry. Somberly, he went into the shop and took the boards that RB helped him crosscut for his wood project, and stacked them outside with the scrap wood he used in the fire pit- the wood project abandoned.

22 GOD GIVE ME WATER

RB traveled some distance when daylight started to fade. As he meandered along the river had become wide and shallow and then narrow and swift in many different places. The water was stained amber brown in color. As RB looked at it, it reminded him of Sawmill Man's wood formula drink. RB then changed his thought of it to be that of a tea created for the nature of Aqua Caverness that was formed from the leach of many different types of stones and fallen leaves.

On the left shore a little brown and furry animal saw that RB was approaching. As RB was traveling up the river against the current, he came near the animal that was mysteriously standing on its two hind legs. It was a Furlucci. His boat became tangent to the Furlucci and it looked at him and his boat again with its beady dark eyes that were obscured by prickly fur. Its jaw jutted forward twice and it dove in the water. It started swimming to RB's boat. It then turned and swam alongside RB as he traveled in his boat. It swam along him for some time. Its pointed nose and wedge shaped head seemed to be in harmony with the water as a wake of small ripples streamed outward behind it with nary a sound. RB wondered why it swam along side, *"Is the Furlucci captivated by the sight of motion of my boat? Did the motion of my boat spur a competitive nature in the Furlucci to race with me? Or did the Furlucci just like to swim alongside me for a sense of camaraderie in this otherwise lonely wild?"*

The Furlucci then swam ahead of RB's boat as if it was in a race with him. "A race with a Furlucci," RB softly mused aloud and maintained his constant speed. The Furlucci paddled quickly, it looked to the left, to see how fast RB's boat was going. Then it paddled some more and looked up at RB. Then it paddled quicker than RBs boat and gained a lead on him. A few boat lengths ahead of RB the Furlucci swam to a stretch of rocky shore and crawled up on the flat surface of a rock just above the waterline. It then stood up on its hind legs and moved its left hind leg in front of its right and then back to where it started. RB laughed aloud, as it looked like it was performing some type of dance. Then while still standing on its hind legs it moved its front paws upward to the right as if pointing to the sky. Then it swept its front paws down past its belly and towards the water's edge on its lower left. Then back up to the right towards the sky again. It did this several times and then disappeared as it scrambled behind some rocks.

RB marveled at the sight of the Furlucci. The motions it had made lessened the sense of loneliness RB had on his journey. The scene of its dance replayed in RB's mind and lent RB a renewed sense of vitality. *"Pointing this way and that all kooky like,"* RB thought and smiled to himself endearingly.

The right shore was a steep high rock faced wall. Some of the rocks of the wall face showed distinct layers. Some of the layers had protruded as rounded outcroppings that hung over the river. RB thought, *"It interesting to see the way water, slime, light and the polish of time have made them unique in their formation."* To him they were like solid formations of personality and character and yet with a sense of permanence- as they were indeed rock. RB saw how in some spots there were little pockets of land at the base of the steep rock face that lined this stretch of the river. *"I do not know this place and if I were to moor on a small pocket of land like that and expected to make my way up to the mesa of the thinly forested and steep rock face I might be out of luck. If for some reason my boat lost its moor while I was scouting around I might be doubly out of luck for good."* RB then pondered how seeds found a place to take root and form into trees in such a rock faces. *"They must have struggled to survive by forming and wedging their ever growing roots into the crevices of the rock face."* As he looked at the vibrant green leaves of the trees, he then wondered how hard it would be for the trees to obtain their nutrients for growth. *"Do minerals wash to their roots from eroding rocks? Do they obtain nutrients from seepage and leaching of the bluff above or do they absorb them from the water table that elevates from the river?"*

As he looked up at the bluff he saw a bird of prey soaring high up in the air. It had a wide wingspan and seemed to be able to fly in any direction while using little of its own effort. He watched it coast and then rise, and wondered how long it took the bird to learn to fly like that. *"It probably did not have that learning at birth or when it was first coaxed from its nest. It is moving in an odd circling pattern utilizing the air currents, what is it looking for?"*

He then came upon another small pocket of land at the base of the rock face. A half dozen Cornfield Birds had climbed down a rocky and steep path that led to the water's edge. *"If I absolutely had to I could probably walk or climb up that to the top,"* he thought. Birds at the back of the gaggle made their way into RB's passing view. They held tight on their descent and he heard their talons, on the ends of their skinny stick legs, clap on rock surfaces. They then pecked at the water's edge for a drink and around the little shore area for the little things they ate. *"If I camp near here overnight it could prove to be unpredictable if the water level were to rise my shoreline campsite would be lost to the steep rock face. Many a people have been lost to the shifting temperament of water that floods on this planet. May I not be one of them!"*

RB then came upon an island in the middle of the river. He looked up on the island and for a brief moment he saw a Gruntoe. A Gruntoe was a four legged animal with a mixture of patches of short brown, black and tan fur. It was created to move fast through the forest, with narrow muscular legs and a lean and taught torso. If need be it could jump great distances to escape a predator. The Gruntoe looked at RB, its ears perked up in RB's direction, and it bound off into the forest of the island.

"She might have liked me just for that little time. Maybe she is really like her two older sisters. She might have a dark side. What could it hurt if I asked her to marry me? If I get back I will have to ask her to be my wife," RB decided as he thought about Tamarack.

Past the island on the left shore of the river was a large area of dried riverbed. Lightly packed tan sands and clay stretched for a great distance. As the river narrowed, on the shore he saw a brown Horloff with a white face. The Horloff was thin in its ribs and its face looked like one of the saddest things he had ever seen.

For some reason the image of the Horloff made him think of women when they were sad. He once saw an aging spinster stand on the side of a village dance when he was young. As he thought about her he wondered if she only knew of the bad things in life and not true love. Seeing the sad faced Horloff he did not know whether to cry in pity for it or laugh as some would say it was the cause of its own circumstances. Some odd sense of learning had told him from experience that if he were to cry, a rainstorm would come and pock and pelt not just the planet but, him in his boat also. He knew the sign as he had come to recognize the pattern and therefore knew not to cry. He then thought of Tamarack and how he would hate to see her be such a spinster some day.

From his boat he saw scattered small tracks from birds and animals in the dry riverbed that formed the left shore. For some reason, RB always found the pattern of bird tracks very comical, if not heartening as if he could see the indecision they took in their little walking journeys. *"A dry river bed can never be thought of as a dry riverbed as even the slightest rain can flood it and below the surface the muck is often very soft and deep,"* he philosophized.

This had been a long and exhausting day for RB, and the chill of the damp night had started to ensue. He had left Sawmill Man's place earlier and had carefully navigated a long distance through stretches of river with fast current.

It was getting dark and cold and a sense of displacement or of being lost started to overtake RB as he could not seem to find a spot to shore his boat to rest the night through. As he motored on in the moonlight, his boat started to graze the bottom of its hull on sandbars hidden just under the surface in the dark of night. After he passed over the first one he hoped it might have been an anomaly but after going some distance he heard the scraping sound again. The sound cleared as he quickly passed over it.

The night air was cold and he needed to sleep soon. He would have to find a place to beach his boat in order to be free from any changing currents that might occur in the dark; changes that might put him in peril if he slept on the water. He needed to find a place fast.

He motored on cautiously in the dark night as he traveled against the current when all of a sudden he heard it again, the jarring sound of his boat running high on a sand bar.

RB grabbed his newly made pole staff secured to the left inside of his hull and attached the blunt like end to it. He had formed the end to it from two blades of an old propeller. He designed it to pivot on the narrow ends of the blades at the end of the pole. And he resurfaced the blades to resemble the webbing from the feet of a Paddlequack Bird. The flared blunt end lessened it sinking into the sand and gave the pole more of a base to push against. Also as he retracted the pole the blunt he formed from the flared blades was made to collapse at the pivot. Therefore it could be brought back to bear more quickly for successive pushes on sand bars.

Determined to survive, in the cold darkness, he stuck the push pole into the sand bar of the river and commandingly yelled "God give me water!" He put his weight into it and the boat moved forward just a little.

All of a sudden his neck stiffened up. He heard the words, "Get used to it," from a scorching brat like voice in the distance. He felt as if it was defying him to live. The wretched tone rasped his ear drums, being more of an annoyance or a distraction to his fight for survival. An intrusion into his individual being it mocked his existence. He pulled his staff back to him and then struck again into the water, and pushed.

"Get used to it." He heard as his whole head seemed to vibrate as if being filed. He was now exhausted and drained of life.

"Get used to it!" He heard again.

He breathed shallow and stuck his staff in again. His fight for freedom to live or submit to death had started and the choice was his.

"Get used to it!" He heard the voice from a young spoiled soul and was voided again.

"Get used to it!" grated him again.

His kidneys were drained of adrenalin and he was far away from any known other "people".

"Get used to it."

The spirit mocked him and he inched on against it, the current and the grasping and holding bottom of sand.

He stuck his pole staff in again, there was very little life left to him.

"Get used to it!" The voice shook his head and almost displaced his self being.

The current had grown strong and sharp rocks lined the shore. The voice mocked him and he was shaking cold and hungry. Even though he had eaten food earlier he seemed to have received no energy from it. He was getting damp in the chilling cold dark and he had no idea where safety lie. But one thing was certain he was not going to go backwards, he would not lose any progress that he fought for.

"Get used to it!" His head vibrated- teeth and bones shaken.

"Get used to it!" The spoiled voice said more quickly as if he missed it the first time.

Weak, as if he could cry, RB stuck and pushed. His fight for survival would not let him succumb to crying.

"Get used to it!"

The boat now veered sideways to the force of the current threatening to take away his hard earned pole pushing work, his progress, and he would not stand for it.

He pushed and then yelled, "God give me water!"

He pulled the slack of his staff up and yelled, "God give me water!" as he exhaled.

His back had no more muscle so he tried to keep it straight to keep from injuring himself.

"Get used to it!" a relentless begging for his life.

"God give me water," he said. His voice would be heard over that of the ephemeral demon.

"God give me water!" The man of ancient origin said as he exhaled, while sticking his pole in the bottom and pushing. "I will defy the false deity!" he was the anger held in thought.

"God give me water!" he bellowed again and thought, "My will is stronger than yours!"

"God give me water!" Again he stuck into the bottom sand muck and gravel with his push pole and this time put the full weight of his balance into it. One slip now and he would be in the cold fast current of the river.

The disembodied soul seemed to descend to him and superimpose his body while it then weakened and taunted him, "Get used to it!"

He could feel the spirit try and possess him and his neck started to stiffen even more and he resisted and kept strong of knee as he pushed on the surface mass of Aqua Caverness that held him.

"God give me water!" He said with his breath.

He stuck, weighed in and it seemed to push a little faster.

"God give me water!" he said, in fury and hope, and pushed.He moved faster now. Was he starting to win against the scraping force of gravity on the bottom of his hull?

"God give me water!" he yelled in a fierce and beastly voice stabbed his pole into the bottom and pushed.

"God give me water!" he was developing a tempo.

"God give me water!"

"God give me water!"

He was free of the bottom and pushed faster.

In this game of life and death today he would not lose.

He struck his staff more fiercely now, bludgeoning and puncturing the planet that had forsaken him.

"God give me water!"

He grabbed his staff tighter. Like a vice, his callous hands would not slip. His grip of life would not be broken as he pushed into the now slightly deeper bottom surface.

His rule of thumb in life was that once he grabbed hold of something, both it and he were safe. He would summon the energy of all the stars in the heavens to hold his life's grip. This is how he lived. He was stronger than odds and made things that were strong. His staff would not waiver.

"No element of Aqua Caverness will defeat me!" he thought in confidence.

His anger fought the voice to its end in eternity.

"God give me water!" he barked.

He imagined the voice broken, a face of it paled to white, drained of most life by his defiant will to survive over the weaker grip it tried to form around him.

His senses diminished to a vague notion of himself and his surroundings.

Of his pole staff he wondered, *"Had the sappy fish gut and insect spirit that held it together taken life in disembodied entity form and was it that that mocked me?"* He already felt that wasn't the true answer.

The coldness that inset into his flesh reached deep into his bone. It was no longer him sticking and pushing, but his skeletal framework that was pushing aside from him, ignoring a now absence of muscle. He was vaguely present and his bones were doing the work.

"God give me water!" He said as he exhaled and then bellowed inward cool fresh night air in order to ease the heat in his lungs, this in defiance of the cold already present in his body.

Uncertain of progress to God or demon he would not lose.

"Let it be demons' fate to die tonight and not mine," he raged in thought.

He summoned the spirit to his staff.

"My bones are not my muscle," he realized.

His night eyes told him aim right, he did and pushed.

The current lessened, and he pushed fast, a safe distance forward the water in the channel slowed and he shored his boat securely. He grabbed two woven blankets of the leather of Horloff that the Worblers had put in his boat before he departed and found some dry firm ground higher up. He lit a small fire and ate some leftover Carpetti fish he brought with him from Sawmill Man's saw mill. He then wrapped up in the cross woven blankets and started to pray, "God thank you…"

23 THE DIRTY RIVER

He awoke the next morning and headed upstream again as he continued his journey home. He approached a fork in the river when he heard a Paddlequack bird squawking. It was flying in the same direction as his boat was motoring in as it approached from behind. When it was directly overhead he looked up at it. As he watched it fly it squawked again and gathered its right wing inward. It squawked a second time and gathered its right wing inward again as it flew to the channel on the left side of the fork. *"I have never seen a Paddlequack fly that way,"* RB thought as the Paddlequack continued to squawk as it flew upstream above the left fork of the river.

RB took the fork that led to his right and after awhile he came to an area of water that was riddled with scattered dead tree limbs and partially submerged logs. He recognized that it would be hard to navigate through. The water was slowly moving, as if it had little pulse left.

On the shoreline scampered a small and furry disheveled looking creature that had dirty prickle hair hackles on its back and cloudy looking eyes. RB focused on it intently and followed it with his eyes. *"It is indeed a Furlucci,"* he realized.

RB leaned over the side of his boat and stuck his hand in the water and when he brought it out, it smelled like sewage. RB looked up and the Furlucci had stopped running and was on a rock. It stood on its hind legs and stared at him in his boat. The Furlucci slowly tilted to its side and fell down. It quickly got back up, briefly looked at RB, and then turned and scampered off.

Still looking to shore RB saw debris caught in bent over and short flattened reeds that were covered with silt like dirt.

As he slowly moved forward in his Skipper a watchman's light on a broken tower came into his view. The light dangled from its broken rest, like something no one wanted to repair for fear of curse or execution.

A short distance later the shore looked void of natural animal life.

Branches long ago burnt were stacked into cones and now marked the settlement grounds. *"To serve as a warning?"* RB wondered. Scattered remnants of clothes littered the landscape. Sun bleached skulls with smashed out holes strewn here and there dared him to look at them. Near the bones lay a pile of junk, wanton of scratching him and leading to his death from whatever its poison was. Clothes hung on branches to dry were bleached and tattered by the times of sun. What Sawmill Man said about Pengavilly had made him curious. Solemnly he beached the tip of his boat to the muck shore and tied it off. He then got out in order to have a look around the site. As he looked around he became somewhat weakened from what he saw at this place.

A tear formed in RB's eye as he saw one little purple flower growing, amid all the death, in the center of the common.

Slowly he walked around the waste land and tried to avoid becoming contaminated from the germy mud of death. Unfortunately he slipped as he stepped on a tree branch and in order to prevent himself from falling ended up stepping in some of the mud. He wanted to wash it off right away but realized that he couldn't, because the dirty water was just as bad. As he walked slowly and more carefully he saw a pair of skeletons in the stagnant shallows; they were white as the eroded tree roots. Man or woman, who would want of tell. He smelled the faint stink from a frothing white formation floating on the surface of the river as a gentle wind blew it near. He walked by shoreline trees that were dusted with stinking silt. He hopped over a pile of jagged rocks. A foul odor emanated and rose from deep within their crevices. *"Something that could bite me likely resides here."* He looked outward from shore again and realized a sudden fear. For if he were to end up wading chest high in the viral brown water he would likely become sick or worse, if he were to sink in it he would die.

A mass of bent and tangled roots exposed through erosion at the water's edge seemed to invite him to climb on them and then fall in a web of potentially broken limbs, his own, only to then be held firm in a chaotic growth. To then die within the trappings of slowly passing death water.

A yellow faced Carpetti fish surfaced near RB. He looked at its mouth as it puckered and pulled the morbid water through its gills. It reminded him of a kissy face. *"No place for you to be either,"* he thought as he saw the heavy and resistant shallow breaths of the fish as it labored to stay alive.

The same species of trees that were naturally found elsewhere were unable to muster the slightest vibrancies of color in this waste land. Permanently they were held frozen by their roots in the darkly disturbing muck. Carefully he stepped and made it past them before he came to another series of exposed roots in which he saw the skeleton of a person. An ankle had apparently twisted and caught, as RB had imagined could happen earlier.

The smell of the place made RB wish for better days.

The shadows of the branches on the filthy water posed a morbid reflection he wanted to deny for what it told of the former inhabitants.

The brush he walked through cast a fragrantly disturbing and finely particulized odor upwards, as if the dead were giving him an unwanted welcome they give to newcomers. *"No animal that relied on its nose could last here,"* RB thought.

A circle formation of rocks and log seats made him wonder if the former residents of the morbidly quiet land longed to sacrifice.

"You'd think God himself had hailed vomit here," he felt.

He looked from the land to the water again. Tiny and odd unexplained bubbles were welling up to the surface in the slow current as it churned. RB didn't want to stand near it and try to convince himself of the cleansing effect of nature here. The vapor of the water lingered close to the surface and was deadening to his eyesight and numbing the front of his face and head.

"Who left a ruin like this?" he looked at an abandoned tent made of tattered sacks and garden plot formations untenably covered with tangled weeds.

"The smell of dead things seems to have permanence here. I would dread to meet a person of this origin." He then came upon one dead fish on the shore of mud. It was lying on its side and missing the eye that looked upward. The open cavity of its belly was rotted past its ribs.

He looked again in question of the stagnant brown water and then walked to center of the village.   There was a tombstone and it read, "Because of their mothers' pity, we lost our greatest city."   From what RB could surmise this was indeed Pengavilly or the ruins of it.   And it was how Sawmill Man implied they be, *"Not knowing how to truly provide for themselves their land became one rattled with waste and uninhabitable, they had no place to go and most died in their filth. Poetic justice for those who made the one they owed everything to suffer."*

RB saw all of this and thought of fragments of phrases from a story that his father had told him and the story formed in his mind.

"After that there was a great flood that came and washed all the remnants of them away. Their coveted land would never be the same. The flood would cleanse and filter the water of the waste through the land it flooded. After awhile the land rose in low spots of the oceans to balance the planet. As it rose the planet became one of turmoil. No more oceans, it became called "The Path of Water" Because that is the path water took to clean the living world, and the planet is now covered by paths of water and not large reservoirs.   The path of water cleansed the world of their jealousy."

RB never knew his mother as she died soon after his birth. His father never talked much about her.   When RB was old enough to fend for himself his father mysteriously disappeared.

RB then remembered when his father first showed him the emblem of their compass rose.   It was the same as the one he saw on the cavern walls and the same one worn by the Worblers.   *"Was my father of mysterious great family lineage in the planets history or was he a pariah or outcast here?"* He wondered.

24 SAWMILL MAN'S PARTING LETTER

RB then came to three monoliths with words, of small letters, inscribed on them. They were raised upright in the center of the village. He stared at them as a whole. One had the mark of a shovel blade on it. He stood there and thought, *"Could these be what Sawmill Man found buried in the ground just before he left Pengavilly? The shovel mark seems to suggest they were buried like what Sawmill Man said. If this is true, why? Why were they hidden only for Sawmill Man to come upon by accident? They seem to be of ancient origin by the style and workmanship of the lettering. Therefore they must have been raised upright and displayed more recently- after Sawmill Man left?"* RB read the first one,

> *"Of the Father*
>
> *You don't want to admit that it is true, because it would be a great source of shame. When you are ashamed of who you are it condemns me.*
>
> *Do not be ashamed your mothers picked a good man.*
>
> *You learned in the best way possible and I have full faith and confidence in you.*
>
> *If there was one thing that was a creation of God in this world, it was that you learned in this way through a good man.*

Do not be ashamed my sons, for when you are, it condemns me. You have nothing to be ashamed of if you were raised differently than others you meet. Your mothers and fathers did this for you because they loved you.

Do not be ashamed because when you are it condemns me. Have confidence in your work and do not fear for me, when I am away.

Do not be ashamed. Be proud for who you are and where your skills came from. Take pride and love in your work and love your creator as your father.

The father of your soul is proud of all of you. Do not be ashamed of your skills or those of your many fathers. Treat your fathers with respect and your sons will then treat you with respect.

Your mothers wanted you to be like me because they loved you and me.

Many of you are like me so don't be afraid to admit that you are also like me.

Do not hate the father of your soul. For I never knew I was. Today I do know and I am not ashamed to admit it. Learn to live independent from me. Let me recognize you through your good deeds and works and that will honor me."

Monolith two read:

"Of the Mother

Your father loved to work as you do. Your father loved to work with his hands and tools and later in life to write stories for you. He loved to think how he could teach others like you do. He loved to learn a new skill, art or science, and whether you know it or not, so do you.

Learn to remember your skill by thinking about them. If you do this you will not be one who "Knows not what he does."

Think of how you mastered your art and what words you could use to describe it, so that anyone could learn it through those words.

Think of things you know of that are not of hand work, think of what words you could use to tell of them so that anyone could learn of such truths.

Thoughts of this nature and knowledge of handwork are not like day and night but more of the same colorful spectrum of the world.

If you can not admit to what you will do, do not do it. He did not ask to be your father and now that it is done and known do not be ashamed of how you learned. Do not seek to destroy your father. Learn, improve and grow as a person from your knowledge.

Your father stood against the souls of medicine men, men of legal matters, priests, savage chiefs, city officials and other leaders of the planet for the good of you and the world. Consider it an honor you are of him."

Monolith three read:

"Of You

Those of you who learned through thiefdom do not seek to covet the knowledge you attained. And do not teach through thiefdom for this steals from the heart of what makes us good. Repent and share your knowledge with heart and not thiefdom. Be a disciple that learneth out of concern for others. Share knowledge and teach from heart out of concern for others. Teacheth so those who are not of thiefdom learneth and not just those of thiefdom. Do not teacheth so that some disciples learn to the detriment of other disciples. If you are of thiefdom yeah will findeth that your best disciples are of the heart.

Teacheth those of thiefdom not by distracting but by demonstrating. If thyne are of thiefdom do not feel your disciples are also.

Master what thou teacheth because only when you have mastered the skills that you teacheth can you think in terms of how to teach. A disciple of heart and learning knows when you have mastered a skill and know what you are teaching and such a disciple will not ask you a question he knoweth would prevent you from teaching. Leaveth the discipline of disciples to the village elder.

Teacheth what you know to be true and why you know it to be true. Teach with your heart and firm stance.

If you teacheth in this manner you hath built a basis of understanding for reason and advancement. To teacheth otherwise leadeth to ruin by disciples of thiefdom who attained power."

After RB read the tablets he thought of a story his father told him once, his father called it the Old Oliver Shorecat story.

"Old Oliver shorecat got mad and clawed a cut in his masters leg and his master reacted by expelling him into the wall with a sweeping broadside kick.

Old Oliver then went on the prowl looking for a fight down by the river. He crawled into a brown woven sack two other shorecats were in. There was a commotion and a young cat came running out of the bag and old Oliver shorecat chased it under a discarded Horloff hide chair.

Snarls were heard and scratching and clawing sounds. Hair was seen flying out from under the chair.

Only one shorecat came out from under the chair, and it wasn't Old Oliver."

RB then remembered the moral his father told him, *"Do not seek to injure your master. And sometimes those who are expelled are the saviors of those that are also condemned, sometimes unintentionally by their last actions."*

25 THE GOOD BOOK

RB walked up to the 'house' on the hill. It was made of stones stacked together with mortar. The front door had long been missing and RB walked to the stone arch where it would have been. "Anybody here?" he yelled into the front room. He waited and yelled again, "Hello. Anyone here?" No-one answered so he walked into the front room. On a pedestal in the middle of the room was a book.

He dusted off the cover and the title read, "The Good Book." He opened it to the first page and as he started to read. After he read the first sentence he realized that he was no longer reading but rather listening to the words written in the book as he turned the pages.

"The Water Spirit was the first life on Verdetia. In happiness it trickled and gurgled. Happily it swam to and fro in the free clean water God had provided for it.

It saw that much around it looked like it, but was not the same as it, in that it did not enjoy the water like it did.

One day it looked around it to see dark plankton like ash descending to the basin of its domain.

Eons passed on Verdetia and much change had happened, but once again the water spirit swam freely in the renewed blessing of God.

When the water cleared it decided that there should be more like itself. The water spirit then said, "May all the clear blue water on Verdetia be happy just like me!"

Great rolling waves of enthusiasm then danced together on its surface.

***

She ruled for a very long time on Loonofur and was smugly satisfied with her role.

Many men indeed became like her and the cold hollow voice that whispers in the wind and mocks goodness.

Her fault was that she cared little for where she lived as her realm was the howling of the spirit world, because that is from where she governed.

She awoke one summer morning and noticed that flowers no longer bloomed. She missed their beauty in her dying world. She summoned and enslaved all remaining men and women on Loonofur and with the daunting fear of persecution and death she commanded them, "Construct a Metal Flower for me!"

When some refused, the coldness of her froze them solid and the howling gale force of her voice then eroded them to dust.

But bitterly she continued on her quest to create beauty in the world to replace what was no more. And Metal Flower was completed.

She awoke and looked outside as the sun reflected on its shimmering petals and stalk. Only the finest gold and silver plating were the showcase finish of her "Metal Flower."

Once again she was pleased and stated aloud to all on she governed, "I have conceived great beauty again on Loonofur. I have brought you my creation of Metal Flower."

The grailing wind from her lungs made rising and falling tones that creaked as it blew over the petals and stem of Metal Flower and she declared of them, "Music to my ear's!" and further rejoiced with her new found talent of song.

The next day she awoke to a freezing world. All the water on the Loonofur had flash frozen solid in preparation for ice drift redevelopment of Loonofur. The true God of creation had returned and had taken one look at her and what she had done. And commanded, "May 'Metal Flower' remain unharmed as all around you it tilled anew, by the mammoth glaciers of my tears- from your coldness."

*"****

A glacier approached the She Spirit as she stood admiring Metal Flower. "I must do something quickly or the glacial drift will destroy my creation!"

Aloud she said, "The God of creation has forsaken me. He now wants to destroy my 'Metal Flower'!"

"What can I do to preserve its beauty!" she asked herself.

With the hand of her wind she uprooted 'Metal Flower' and then she road it like a sleigh.

In the wake of her sleigh many grey chasms were carved.

Her solitude on the Loonofur was now echoed by the thrill of her till as she heard the sound from the death of her tines circle around the Loonofur to greet her again.

She rejoiced in screeching wretched happiness as she rode her 'Metal Flower' sleigh until it was brought to a deadening dullness on Loonofur.

She stood up and looked around her and saw that she had ruined 'Metal Flower'!

Then her spirit shrieked and imploded. The entropy from it flowed chaotically in the hollow and void ashen grey crevices that had formed as she rode the beauty of Her creation.

Its thin stream of ash seemed to be searching frantically and inescapably in the gravity that bound it, lost to the horizon!

*"****

Her Loonofur had always orbited around another planet~ Verdetia. She was not content to be alone, her spirit reconfigured to a oneness so that she could howl and scream from her now dead world to the planet that she orbited. A man lived on the planet and she howled and yelled to him. His name was Lord Uriah and every time she yelled at him the needle on his compass spinned and he became confused and disorientated.

One day Lord Uriah looked up in the night sky and said, "Do not yell at me anymore!" Somehow she heard him from across the distance of space between the planets and this pleased her. She then proceeded to tell everyone on the Verdetia what to do as she sat on her dead world.

What she did not know was that when she yelled at him all the compasses in heaven also became hay-wired.

One day as she yelled at Lord Uriah, God decided that was enough! God saw what she had done again and an unbalanced asteroid carommed onto a course to obliterate her dead world.

Lord Uriah's compass needle started to turn in frantic circles on its dial. Lord Uriah then became confused and felt lost in life. Lord Uriah was not lost for very long before he saw the asteroid in the daytime skies as it was headed straight for Loonofur. The rogue asteroid hit Loonofur and Loonofur exploded into a mass of dust and water.

As the ice core of her planet fragmented and dispersed a massive cloud of dust and water were caught in the gravitational field of the larger planet that Lord Uriah lived on~ Verdetia. The skies of his planet darkened and the rain started to pour. It continued to rain until the planet was completely flooded.

The planet flooded and Lord Uriah died. The white light of his spirit traveled through the dark light matter of the universe. The dark light was everywhere and enveloped the white light of his soul. But the dark light could not impede his progress because it had no choice but to make way as the white light of his soul was pushed forward because the dark light in front of him was always anxious to get out of his way. The true nature of the dark light is that of a follower therefore its reality will always be to yield to the course of the white light. That is how the white light always finds good places to go to. They are places the dark light avoids like it does the white light it envelopes. That is also how the good soul took residence over a fertile green and blue planet. And a new seed of change was planted that offered hope for the world to develop into a divine creation.

'***

"She tells those on Verdetia what to do from her dead moon!" RB thought in sadness as he summarized the gist of the story.

There was a shelf under the pedestal that held The Good Book. On it were several more of the same 'The Good Book' RB noticed as he thought there was nobody who would find any missing.

RB then got back in his boat and solemnly traveled onward. The river channel started to widen again and the lake he had foreseen revealed itself. The distant shore could not be seen on the horizon. The crystal blue water and the white cloudiness seen at a distance created a shimmering silver line that transitioned the water from the sky. This would invite his path. Keeping his bearing straight he headed into open water toward the beauty of that glistening transition of unknown. He would not be afraid of a natural beauty like this as some were, because he felt an origin of oneness with this horizon.

With no meaningful reference aids to navigation, he was intuitively confident in the spot on the horizon he chose and headed to it.

He reached the far unfamiliar shore as daylight turned to night, anchored to shore, and wrapped in his Worbler blanket. As he started to drift to sleep he queried his boats computation and control system, "Cauldron One please initialize a scan of heavens for relative position to delta homeward coordinate."

Ships systems replied, "You're not too far off RB. It is a short distance on shoreline to the port side. Too short to mention."

RB replied, "Save celestial reference scan and make inherent to further relative position course. And don't forget to initiate and coordinate with gyroscopic compass."

"***

RB awoke to daylight and a small chop of water that clapped to shore. He then heard the motor of his boat start up.

He opened his eyes further to see that two Mud Sticker birds were in his boat. One of the Mud Sticker birds was plopped in RB's driver seat. It was resting back on its plump round mid section and had its feet perched on the steering wheel. RB watched in amazement as the bird then grabbed hold of the throttle with its pointy mud covered beak and pulled back on it. The boat started to motor forward! *"The Mud Sticker is driving my boat away!"*

"Shoo, shoo." RB yelled at the Mud Stickers as they took off in his boat.

"Cauldron One! Cauldron One! Return to shore immediately…Cauldron One! Return to shore immediately!" The Cauldron indicated its intent to comply as it slowed down and then turned one hundred and eighty degrees- in the direction of RB at shore.

As the boat started to move in the direction of shore the Mud Sticker in the seat stood up on its long legs, flapped its wings and flew up off and away from the deck of RB's boat. The second Mud Sticker then followed it in flight.

When the boat reached shore RB took a towel wiped off the seat and regained his composure.

He started his journey homeward again. The scenery started to become more familiar to him and a sense of ease returned to him.

He traveled quickly and in the fast approaching distance he saw water cascading over and down the face of a waterfall, the same one that led to his demise.

For a reason unknown to him his boat sped up and was headed straight to the rock face of the falls. RB started to well up with anxiety when a voice on his boats control interface broadcast a message, "RB this is Beesil Worbler, I anticipated your need upon approach to the falls you described and interpolated the proper technology into your boat to overcome them. Hold fast and tight RB."

RB grabbed a tight hold of his hull. A force, like that of sphere, secured items as it held them firmly in the boat.

Beesil's command instructions continued, "Engine ballast weight to aft section. Repellence section fore. Tilt with full thrust. Scoop to intake fore gravity displacement water. Initiate creation of nose vacuum displacement. System rate algorithm control to overcome gravity based vertical water force."

RB and his boat climbed the falls and eased onto the surface of the river above as he looked around in amazement.

This was home.

26 THE RETURN OF OLD JOSEY

When Medika and Shurlene took their revenge against Old Josey he had billowed high and away and too, was seemingly lost in the air.

Old Josey looked down at the world below as he had never seen it before. High up in the sky he was thirsty and tired as the wind was drying him out. Tethered to the oneness of balloons he had all but given up hope until a Crockus bird flew near him.

"What are you doing up here," The Crockus bird said.

"I didn't know Crockus birds could talk," Old Josey replied.

"What are you doing up here," The Crockus bird said again.

"Somebody attached this to me and I floated up here," Old Josey replied.

"What are you doing up here."

"I told you somebody attached this balloon to me."

"What are you doing up here."

"I am not supposed to be up here, an evil Mayhem did this to me."

"What are you doing up here."

"Is that all you can say?" asked Old Josey.

"What are you doing up here," the Crockus bird said again.

"What are you doing up here," the Crockus bird said again.

At this point Old Josey reached out and grabbed the bird by its momentarily closed beak. He had taken in the slack of the line and, with the long beak in hand, punctured a small hole in the balloon near where the tether was tied. With a downward motion of his hand he thrust the Crockus bird away.

"Who kicked me from the nest. Who kicked me from the nest. Who kicked me from the nest," the Crockus bird was heard saying as it tried to regain control of its flight.

Old Josey grabbed the balloon around the hole he created. He then got his bearings and through a controlled motion of releasing air from the balloon made a glide path to where he thought the choir would be on shore.

27 MEDIKA AND SHURLENES RECKONING

Once on Upper Falls section of the Cauldron River, RB taxied his Skipper to Medika and Shurlenes' pier only to see the two in single piece bathing garments with Pepper sitting obediently nearby.

He walked up to the two sisters and said to them, "What is the matter with you two? You could have killed me."

The two looked at each other in astonishment and then laughed.

"We already thought we did," Medika, still the same, said.

Medika then came charging at him, as she swung her fists she spewed these words at him, "I think I will right now sissy." RB in turn picked her up and heaved her lock, stock and Horloff barrel in the river. Shurlene came at him also.

Quickly RB got behind her and locked his arms around her chest. He lifted her off the ground and started to carry her to the river's edge.

"You're gonna pay for this!" she said as she started to buck.

"You have too much hatred boiling inside you!" RB said.

Shurlene bucked again and said, "You better show some respect!"

"You Mucklum slimes have no respect for anyone and resent having to work or think," RB scolded.

"You don't know who you are dealing with," she said. As she then bucked upward to free herself from RB's hold on her, he took the opportunity when her feet were off the ground to run her straight into the river.

The women got out of the water and looked like their jaws had grown forward, resembling those of grass chewing Horloff's. Their faces were still and flat with rage. Their eyes not humanlike; but more of the furied instinct of an animal.

They straightened up their single piece bathing garments and Shurlene said, "I'm real live mad at you!" Medika added at him too, "I'm real live mad at you also."

Medika then grabbed a long gaff hook and proclaimed, "Shurlene let's finally have our way with pretty boy here." Medika started to swing the hook at RB. Shurlene wiped her hands together in cross like fashion while she again savored the moment.

Just then Constable Josey and Tamarack arrived to help RB.

"I'm not square with these two yet either RB," Old Josey quickly said to RB in the midst of the commotion.

The choir members Ms. Randolph, Edora, Ms. Hillsmith and Miss Bellscooper and other community members were coming from all directions to help also. The must have seen RB was home. From a distance the group encircled the two sisters and started walking in closer to them.

"We know what you been up to!" Edora said.

"You were bad all along and you lived right near us," said Ms. Randolph.

"When we're through with you you'll tell us all you done!" Ms. Bellscooper yelled at them.

"We know you're murderers," said Duffy a dweller from up the river.

"We know you're thieves!" said Wilbur Squillbur also from farther up river.

"You don't belong here with us good people!" said Hillsmith, whose neck was in a brace from Medika's blow.

"You belong where you have to fend for yourself and die because you can't!"

"We know you ain't right!" said Wilbur Squillbur.

"You're not getting away with it anymore!" said Old Josey.

"No more easy life for you, you'll pay for what you done now!" screamed Ms. Randolph.

"You're through, you hear me you're through," hollered otherwise mild mannered Ms. Hillsmith. While yelling at the two, for their evil deeds committed, the group closed in on them.

"You're going to be judged by us," said Old Josey.

"We've got a lot of questions to ask you," said RB.

"Were going to be fair with you," said Old Josey.

"You're not taking us anywhere!" said Medika and she and her sister started a swinging.

"Yes we are!" declared Old Josey as he grabbed her fist as she flung it at him.

Ms. Randolph jumped on the back of Medika. Old Josey let go of her hand. And Medika fell to the ground with Ms. Randolph on her back. The gaff hook fell from Medika's other hand and Wilbur Squillbur kicked it away. Ms. Randolph lay on top of her back and held her down.

Shurlene took a mock swing at Old Josey and then dove for the gaff hook. She quickly grabbed the gaff hook up and as she stood it came swinging at Old Josey. RB grabbed it before it got to Josey. Duffy bent down and locked his arms around

Shurlenes waist. Shurlene started to wiggle about to free herself and then fell to her knees. Duffy then pushed forward with his legs and plowed Shurlene into the ground. They then tied her hands together too, while nearby Wilbur Squillbur tied Medika's together.

The two subdued sisters were stood back up on their feet and marched off.

After the commotion died down Helmoot who had tagged along with the choir women and Pepper ran to greet RB.

"Oh my good lads, I missed you so much."

"What was this all about RB," Pepper asked as RB petted him and Helmoot.

"It looks to be over now."

Tamarack joined RB too and said, "I am not like Shurlene and Medika."

"I know you're not," RB replied.

"Cherry and I we searched for you…" RB hugged Tamarack.

"What will happen to them?" she asked.

"They will be locked in the old Horloff pen that we rarely used. Old Josey will make a list of all complaints against them," replied RB.

As RB walked Tamarack home that night he thought, *"I know what will make Tamarack to be happy with me forever; I will make her a brand new boat!"*

"What did you like most about your Cauldron Skipper?" RB asked Tamarack.

"I liked the way that I was up so high while I steered. It really gave me a sense of excitement," Tamarack said.

"That gives me a good idea of how to make a new one for her," RB thought.

"I have hired Wilbur Squillbur to churn Horloff milk for me to barter and trade with others," Tamarack said to RB.

"People act that way to you again and we'll bite them!" Helmoot said to RB.

"Yes we will," added Pepper.

"We'll bite them RB!"

'***

The next day was the day of the trial.

Medika and Shurlene were put up on the center of the platform the choir used as a stage and the community members sat on stump type log stools while they listened to the proceedings.

Old Josey then stood at the podium next to Medika and Shurlene and said, "Medika and Shurlene are accused of attempting to murder RB Rough. RB you tell your side of the story again."

"They went raging nuts and tried to kill me."

"Okay then," said Old Josey.

"You've got no proof of nothing. We run a legitimate business that is an asset to this community. Where would all of you be without our Horloff products? Poor RB, we...." Medika started to cry. "We tried to help him. His boat..." She cried some more. "...was going over..."

"That's not how I remember it," Said Old Josey.

"Well your memory might be a little cloudy. It was RB's contraption that sent you into the sky."

"Well I guess that is true," said Old Josey.

"We were trying to help RB. We knew he lived alone and we are always's concerned for him. Medika and I we grabbed a mooring line and tried to catch RB's boat just before it went over. The boat seemed to malfunction. We had suspected that RB had been using a substance to power his motors that was unsafe, unlike our proper distilled Horloff milk fuels. We tried to prompt him to come forth at the time we first met with him that day. We knew he wasn't trying to cheat because there aren't any rules saying he didn't have to use our Horloff based fuel." Her voice a little higher now, "And he wasn't cordial. And also he was making advances to our little sister Tamarack. It was no secret, by us or others that they weren't meant for each other; he is older, not good enough. His parents were irresponsible and went over the falls. His father fell and cracked his head wide open on a rock."

"How do you know what happened to him? No one knew how it happened, how do you know he cracked his head?" RB asked.

"Well I'm assuming he fell like you did."

"You know very well that's not what happened. Why do you change like this from good to bad to good so quickly," RB asked.

"You're being silly RB," she said.

Old Josey started to look like he would be sympathetic to the sisters, but then got his comeuppance. "You darn near strangled me. She did," Old Josey said as he faced the gathering.

"No. That is not true. RB's contraption fired and you were being lifted in the air, just like what happened to us Josey."

Old Josey rubbed his chin in thought.

"We tried to save you too, but too quickly you…"

"Enough!" said Ms. Randolph, "You threw us all in the water to face a certain peril."

"No, all those lines of deck…you tripped."

"I have to wear this brace from where you punched me," said Hillsmith.

"I know what happened!" said Old Josey. And then he said, "Anyone like to say anything in their defense?" He looked around the crowd and then looked at Tamarack and said, "Tamarack do you support your sisters? You were there too, if they are found guilty of attempted murder, by a vote, you will face the same punishment as them."

"I tried to stop them. I am not a murderer. I have loved RB for some time," Tamarack pleaded.

"Maybe you made a little mistake Tammy, we've fended for ourselves after mom and dad went over the falls," Medika said.

"That wasn't right. I won't resort to that in life," Tamarack replied.

"You're nothing without us, you're not strong enough to do what we do," Medika said.

"She is strongest of all of you," RB interjected.

"I won't be a terror," Tamarack stated.

Medika and Tamarack stared at each other in silence until Old Josey spoke from the podium again, "Does anyone have anything to say in their defense or a story to tell with regards to their guilt."

"Yes I have a story to tell," said Duffy. Duffy was an older man from up river, had thinning hair that streamed the sides of his red scalp. His long gray beard was a shaggy dirt rag. He found the composure to speak;

"One day those sisters insulted my son. I spoke back and told them, 'It wasn't their place to talk to him like that.' They looked at me red faced like I ought not dare question their behavior. But then they calmed down and said they were sorry... They didn't look like they were going to cause any more trouble. And everything seemed like I straightened things out with them. But a few weeks later they sold me some milk. I tasted it and it didn't seem right and said so. They said it was of a different new better flavor. We gave some to our baby and it died. I couldn't put the blame on them but they had a gleam in their eye ever after when I saw them.

There was silence and the community members sitting on the stumps looked sadly at one another.

Then Wilbur Squillbur spoke up, "I've got a story to tell also's." Unsteadily Wilbur walked up to the podium as if his limbs were dried. The scruffy man wore a brimmed reed woven hat, as he looked around at the gathering a small winged bug flew out of his gray beard. He looked like he wondered if he would get in trouble for speaking against them and said, "One time I cleaned and polished my boat. I was all by myself. I got it nice and glossy and worked real hard. I was proud and afterwards stood back and admired my work. While I was doing the work, Medika happened to pass by and said, "I bet you don't know you missed a spot. I said, 'Oh no, I didn't.' She nodded her head twice with a smile as if to say, 'You'll see.' The next day before I went to take my family for a ride I took my boat for a test drive. There was a knurled hole in the side. The boat started to fill with water and sank. The two sisters came to help and said they would pull it up off the bottom. Cherry was just a young girl then, but she was with them. I had seen them working and knew they were strong, more so than some men. They attached a line to my boat and sped up real fast. Then my boat was towed over rocks, they didn't slow down or nothing. No actions as if concerned." His voice more shaking now, "They beached it on a sandy shore, in an alcove somewhere. I couldn't find the place again by myself. They turned the hull over to look at the dents. The other two boats there next to mine were turned hull side up and had fresh foot stomps on them. The girls were threat-some. They rode me home and acted like I had not cause to be mad. I have been scared of them since, but didn't know what to do; I felt I had no rights."

"Anyone else?" declared Josey.

A skinny man with brownish skin and a short cropped gray beard wearing an adventurous looking hat that blended in with the woods was sitting on a stump. He declared he had something to say, by raising his hand in front of him. He shook as if frightened a bit as he spoke from where he stood. His eyes darted nervously with concern. He had a small muffin in his hand. "I've got my story to tell," Lamont said.

"Please state your name for the record," said Josey.

"Lamont."

"Continue."

"One day while I was working on my boat, Shurlene came by, and unasked, offered to help. She said she knew all about mechanical stuff. Had read about it. She said she could help."

Lamont looked around at the people on stumps.

"Please continue," said Old Josey.

"After awhile we were all deep in a muck of parts. And I said, 'Wait, no that's wrong.' But she insisted she knew better and kept a fixing. She did help put it back together. But, I've thought about it in my mind for awhile and this is how I describe it. It was like she was taking something apart and not knowing where the extra piece goes when you put it back together or taking a looking at what you've done for awhile for rationalization sakes and throwing the extra piece to garbage after deciding you don't need it anymore. Now it seemed okay for awhile, my boat that is. The way she fixed it... When we started it up it had a soft groan or roar. Hearing this she smiled like she made it work so well. I said, 'That noise isn't a cause for concern?' She said, 'No, no. It's better that way at first. It will go away after awhile.' She tossed them parts over the side. Well that noise didn't go away, it just got worse. More louder and louder and now it's got a clunk, clunk, clunk."

"Is that the clunk, clunk, clunk we always hear, Lamont?" asked Josey.

Lamont looked up and down and then up again as if ashamed and nodded his head.

"Didn't you say anything to her?" Josey asked.

"Yes, and when I did, she apologized all cordially and told me where I could find some parts to fix it."

"So I took her map and found that same alcove Wilbur talked about. There were Moreloaf bones piled up there and maybe some bones of what looked like us too. I got a little scared and turned back."

There was a silence and the people sitting on stumps looked at each other.

"Anyone have anything to say before we take a vote?" asked Old Josey.

There was a solemn pause at the gathering and then Old Josey spoke again, "We need to talk about what to do so that this doesn't happen again."

"I want my boat back," said Wilbur Squillbur.

"I want to go to Dead Boat Alcove and see what's there," said Lamont.

"We should go to this 'Dead Boat Alcove' and see what's there," said Ms. Hillsmith.

"Yeah that sounds like a good idea," said RB.

"Okay I agree with that. Let's do that then. Who wants to go?" asked Old Josey and the response was unanimous.

"We will de-convene until we go to Dead Boat Alcove tomorrow. Shurlene and Medika will stay at the old Horloff

Mill until then. We'll meet back here at the stumps and podium first light."

'***

The community had spoken with a unified voice, everyone wanted to go and they all got in their boats ready to go. They followed Old Josey in his boat. Wilbur Squillbur and Lamont also went with him. Medika and Shurlene went in Old Joseys boat too, with their hands tied so they couldn't get away. Medika and Shurlene sat silent while the line of boats headed to Dead Boat Alcove.

After some distance then they started to pass a hidden feeder creek on the left and Lamont spoke, "That's the entrance right there."

"No it isn't," Medika said with a scowling tone.

"It isn't the entrance to what Medika?" RB asked coolly.

Silently Medika glared at RB as the boats then made their way into the inlet. When he turned to look at her she said to him under her breath, "You weren't supposed to come back."

"You could figure out a way to kill a person so they were still alive," he coldly replied.

The narrow channel widened out and Lamont pointed in the direction to the left, motioning to Old Josey where to steer. As they made their way around the bend they saw boats turned over upside down on shore just like Lamont and Wilbur Squillbur said. Old Josey counted them quickly there were six boats there and that was three more than what Lamont and Wilbur Squillbur indicated.

"What's the meaning of this," Old Josey said to the sisters while he pointed at all the boats.

"We've never seen this before," Shurlene said.

"That's my boat there. It's been missing for quite some time," said Edora.

All the villagers that gathered that day and made the trip went ashore to look around except Medika and Shurlene.

"That is a pile of Moreloaf skulls! What have you done here?!" Old Josey said.

Medika looked to the right and saw green eyes with fiery red centers staring at her from some thick bushes. The shape of the creatures head was like that of a Moreloaf. The creature's mouth opened and exposed fangs twice as long as that of the average Moreloaf's teeth. Very discreetly Medika nodded her head meaning 'No!' to the creature. It then sunk into the background of the cover and could not be seen anymore.

"You killed these Moreloafs?" asked Ms. Hillsmith.

"I said I ain't never seen those before. Those could be wild bones," Shurlene answered.

"Stacked in a pile? What evil ceremonies went on here? What were you trying to create?" asked Ms. Randolph.

"Okay we have all seen enough. Let's take a vote. Each of you has been given a piece of paper that you can write innocent or guilty on. Please do so at this time," said Old Josey.

'***

The votes were collected and tabulated. Old Josey then gave the verdict in what came to be known as the Mucklum and Horloff trial, "I, as deemed Constable and Commissioner of Waters, have deemed by vote that you have committed a commission of waters type offense. Medika and Shurlene your defense has proven to be inadequate, you are found jointly and severally guilty of attempted murder. You will be stripped of all wealth and banished from the community. You will be transported far away to a place called Swampy Fork Delta. You will be present and view your Cauldron Skippers as they are decommissioned. We'll come back here and have a look around, see what else you done wrong someday."

"Flip the boats over and we will tow them back. If we have to, one boat will be towed back by two of ours via a tow line fore and aft, so be it," said RB.

"I agree," said Old Josey and they solemnly did so and made their way for home.

'***

A pronged siphoning fork was inserted into the fill top of the fuel tank. Medika moaned, "Not my power cider," as the fuel was siphoned away in preparation for obliteration of the boat.

Medika and Shurlene then on looked in horror as the Commissioner of Waters lowered a lifting claw attached toward the end of a crane towards Medikas boat. The claw of the crane enclosed around the engine and was raised via a pulley system.

As the crane lifted the boat up by the engines the weight of the hull tore the hull free from the engines via the force of gravity as it was positioned over the pit. Medika's hull was thus disemboweled of its engines and then fell downward into a lower unseen chamber where old Horloff bones were once crunched up. Medika moaned in horror as her boat, the one she etched three notches in the side of, fell into a crunching chamber out of everyone's sight and was therefore decommissioned.

The crane turned back and the claw extended downward and the fingers of the claw enveloped Shurlene's engines next. Her boat was raised in the air and positioned over the Horloff bone crunching pit. Old Josey pulled the pin that free spooled the winch and the boat fell. Quickly he levered the winch brake and the abrupt stop to the downward force tore the hull from the engines. It was heard crashing into the Horloff bone pit. Shurlene could not contain herself and mewled weakly, "Not my Mooky…not my… Mooky Booky," and broke into frantic tears. The crane moved to the side and the claw released her engines which fell bluntly to the ground.

The two evil sisters, being banished from the community, were stripped of all belongings. They were put on a one way boat fashioned like a prison. It would lead them upstream around a fork in the river and then downstream to what was called South Fork. As they travel down South Fork the water turned to the consistency of an ugly gray pigmented silt, unlike the amber beauty of North Fork Cauldron.

The boats modular command system had been programmed to avoid all waterway obstacles and take them downstream for over one day's worth of swift travel, down the south fork. At which point the captive restraint systems disengaged and Medika and Shurlene were freed. The boats command and control system then self destructed it. The white flash of fire flame on the straight line of the hull split it into two and steam rose at the surface. The hull was breached by a prepositioned electric fuse coil of intense heat. The boat sank in the water and Medika and Shurlene swam with the current to shore.

"What do we do now?" Medika asked.

"We go to Penganuevo."

28 THE RB PROPOSAL

The next day, RB went to the sand pit where he cast the Sirus Mayhem resin for the boats that he made and started to dig and rake a form in the clay like sand that would form the hull of a new boat for Tamarack. Once he had the form dug for Tamarack's new Cauldron Skipper he raked it to remove any odd contours from the hull. He then patted the raked sand clay basin until it was compacted and smooth.

He then got the sealed buckets where he stored the components he kept to make boat hulls with, specifically; sappy dark Horloff Milk, specific strong natural fiber plants, Tucci, and dry hot sands. He spread the dark Horloff Milk according to Sirus Mayhems recipe, placed the specific strong natural plant fibers on the dark sappy milk, basted this with Tucci powder and then with the hot mineral sands. The good once again turned into the translucent green Gritallia and then the Tucci formed the latticework strength of structure as it was taken into the strong natural plant fibers by an osmotic type reaction. RB had just cast a new boat hull for Tamarack. And of course; RB use more refined versions of the original recipe.

As RB builds Tamarack's new boat he infuses it with song;

"A new boat for the one I love.
A new boat to the water I'll shove.
The best way to spend my time.
Is to please a woman mine.
So that she gives me fellow sons.
And daughters, not so gauntly ones.
A new boat for the one I love.
A new boat to the water I'll shove.
I infuse you with a safety song.
So that once afloat nothing goes wrong."

After the hull had mostly cured anxiously RB flipped it out of its mold. He had decided that he would indeed paint gold colored stripes on it to represent what Tamarack meant to him. He was eager to try making a paint that used Horloff extract and the gold pigment from the coppernicus plant. So he thickened the pigment with secret Horloff extract. He stirred the mixture some with the handle of his brush and painted thin copper colored stripes on his hull from bow to stern. After he looked at what he had painted he thought, *"Tamarack is really going to love this!"* Little did RB realize what he had just created at this point in time. He had orientated the hull with such a fashion by the coppernicus powder paint formula that he made that…he had created a hull design that could convert water ions from water into electricity; he had created a Water Voltaic power cell. The water Voltaic cell would also have the ability to collect stray light from under the hull and too; convert it to electricity.

RB then got the idea, "What if I were to entirely swap my Horloff fuel based motors out in favor of electric based concentric drive shaft gradient clutch based ball motors?

187

'***

RB walked Tamarack quietly home while holding her hand. When RB saw Tamarack's home, which she formerly shared with her sisters, he said,

"On my travels I met a sawmill man. He knew much but was all alone in life. I stayed with Worbler's they were a fascinating people. They saved my life and nurtured me back to health. They were the size of children and yet with great capabilities. Tamarack, I want to have a family, with children. I am self reliant, but I need you in my life."

"It is so nice that you are home and safe," said Tamarack.

"Sawmill Man has prepared for a new settlement, he has stockpiled building supplies. He was hopeful for new developments. You should take a trip with me some time to see him and you could also meet the Worblers, who saved me."

"I would love to."

"It is quite some distance but I made it there and back so we can go too."

"It would be nice to go somewhere new."

"Tamarack you have such a lovely singing voice won't you join Old Josey's singing group with me. We sing great together," RB stated.

"RB, I would love that."

"They are having a meetup tonight, to be held on the sandy shore of Ms. Randolph's place. You'll join with me then?"

"Absolutely!" replied Tamarack who gushed with enthusiasm.

'***

"Welcome RB, I am glad you came to listen to us sing tonight," said Old Josey.

"Well actually Josey, we, Tamarack and I, thought we would sing with you."

"That would be wonderful. We are always glad to have new members. Here is our list of songs. But wait since it is a special occasion having you back, why don't we all sing, "Happy Together We Are Now""

Old Josey motioned with a reed to start and all their voices were then heard together.

"Happy together we are now.
It's so good to be with friends.
To share loving memories of river bends.
Happy together we are now.
To be home with people we love.
Free from the push pole shove.
Happy together we are now.
Smiling faces with goodness hearts.
Sharing stories including good parts.
Happy together we are now.
Before the light does fade.
We take pride in the lives we've made.
Happy together we are now.
We share and covet not.
Nor seek against others in plot.
As from the stars we begot.
The sun that warms us hot.
Plants that grow on our lot.
That we pick on our way as we sometimes trot.
And then eat from in our pot.
As this is how we were taught.
Happy together we are now.

Happy together we are now.

Happy together we are now.

Many songs were song that night and after the festivities ended RB walked Tamarack home. After awhile of neither speaking, in mutual peace and respect of each other's company, RB cleared his throat a little and daring to break the silence spoke, "I feel there is something good between us. I have plans to open a saw mill and teach the working crafts I have knowledge of, and those learned recently from the Worblers, that saved my life. Tamarack, I learned from Sawmill Man that I don't want to be alone the rest of my life- that I want to have people around that I love. I learned how to prepare materials in large scale numbers from Sawmill Man. From the Worblers I learned how to cook, I learned how to care for people with a sense of compassion, as they did me."

As they round the bend and pass the last remaining forestry on the left, before home, Tamarack's eyes open wide with loving appreciation as she sees a new Cauldron Skipper with the christening name Tamarack Duce painted across the transom.

"Is that for me?" Tamarack asked with a sense of astonishment.

"With all my heart and soul," RB replied.

In joyful acceptance Tamarack embraced RB and said, "You are so wonderful to me."

RB replied, "You mean the world to me. My outlook on life has changed greatly since I've gotten to know you better. Seeing you every day, by day, gives me something better to live for."

Unable to contain himself he broke into song,

"Tamarack with your polished stony eyes of blue, oh how I wish that we was one from two.

Tamarack with your darkness hair. I'm quite fond of your attractive flair.

Tamarack I love the way we get along and that is the purpose of this song.

With the loving gift to you of the new water carriage. I now ask for your hand in marriage."

RB got down on one knee and continued singing formally:

"That is how I feel us should be. Tamarack will you marry me?"

Not hesitating for an instant Tamarack replied, "Yes." And then continued;

"RB you're the best thing for me. When with you my eye's truly see.

I've cherished the times I've been with you, and long for the ones that are anew.

I never knew what I had missed until it was you that I had kissed.

Today is the happiest day of my life. I have so longed to be your wife."

RB started in, "I'm so grateful you said yes, and confirm my love was not a guess. I will keep you happy each and every day. As we journey together on life's way."

"How proud I am to be with you, as together we live our life anew."

Tamarack broke in, "I'm so proud of you my fellow. And love to hear your commanding voice a-bellow. I know you're the best around and that our voice of love together is quite sound."

RB and Tamarack are married out front of his small home, that he considers a castle, to the melodies of Josey's Barnacle Barrier Choir."

29 WEMBLY WILLOWS AGAIN

RB stated "We've got the race ahead of us today so I'm not going to read you the News of the River Today, but instead, a poem about nature. By the author, let's see what his name is, his name is indeed Wembly Willows, it says right here at the end of it. Wembly Willows, and the title of the poem is "The Mystery of Nature".

Tamarack saw that RB was about to read and lit her cob pipe. RB pretended not to show his disgust for it and started reading the poem.

"*To plant your roots and grow strong in rich soil and varied weather,*

They held strong on the bank and rose from shores. Stubborn to modern development they extended their forestry until they reached the next river.

Strong arms, held aloft and firm, provide shade and cover.

The landscape that forms and shapes from more than one.

Always a subtle difference from yesterday.

A tall tree no longer forming branches, how long will it stand?

The pattern and color of scale present among underwater weeds that stand just as tall.

Rhythmic strides, the beauty of motion and form in nature.

The pattern of fur much like the grain of wood.

Tracks tell us what was here but is not now when we are.

The eyes that see you unaware of them; and scamper away.

Contrasting colors of feathers, no longer shy of you, soon to try their song on your ear.

With wings stretched they breathe the rising air currents.

The changing seasons remind us that we only live one season of transition.

The many forms of transparent water are a representation of this.

The fusion of two forces combine to produce the initial energy or steam, hot abuzz, like the formation of a soul.

For the blessed middle of our lives the stream seems to flow with ease.

The bubbling sound seeming to indicate a joyful purpose. It knows not the reality or our comprehension of flow of time.

Two streams form to create one. Sometimes when split by an island one stream forms two.

As energy wanes only a few days during the year do we feel at parity to the elements, where adaption is not needed. Adjustment, struggle, change and pampering arise as we lose our oneness or unity to atmosphere.

In winter hard and cold and easily broken when thin.

It would seem that time is flowing in an opposite direction to our state of being and awareness with water. Wouldn't we rather swim upstream?"

"Much better than that wicked tortured text you read to us last time, you said, so and so wrote," spouted MSSR Von Helmoot.

"Maybe you have something you would like to read Tamarack," RB said.

"Well, I will see what I can find," She said as she set her pipe down and went to look.

"Conjured up images of my own, meaningful to myself as you read that," Pepper gruffed.

"That is called blank verse poetry," RB told as he picked Tamarack's pipe up and stuck it in his pocket.

Tamarack now arriving from the bedroom, countered, "The poem is too prose like, sounding like exposition not verse."

"Wembly couldn't rhyme," retorted the older of the two MSSR Von Helmoot as he scrunched up his nose.

"It might not been as beautiful if it did," RB sighed. He then walked out to the look at the water at the river's edge and Tamarack followed him.

RB looked at Tamarack and said the fresh air and water is so beautiful. I am so glad you are here with me. They looked in each other's eyes and embraced one another. Closer now, RB kissed her. While doing so he reached in his pocket and tossed her tangleweed smoking cob pipe in the river. She seemed not to notice.

30 THE LAST RACE

"They created enough waste. I saw no reason why we couldn't reuse, what of…the hulls and motors."

"It is not like we were being unfair. They weren't theirs anymore!"

"Didn't we do it shifty like though? The way we turned off the crunching mechanism when their boats were dropped in the crunching chamber?"

"No, wasn't anything shifty about it."

'***

"I ain't never had a boat like this before!" said Smokey Josey as he levered back for more speed.

Bucking his wake as he crossed over it to pull alongside was Wilbur Squillbur who then said, "Me neither, Medika's engines sure did mine good," as he powered forward with a full boat of friends. They were smiling as never before, free of the oppressive behavior of the Mayhem gang.

Today Tamarack was in the lead with RB skirting her wake, close behind.

All boats made the turn at the buoy without incident.

Going into the final stretch it was Tamarack, RB, Cherry Bo Berry, Old Josey and Wilbur Squillbur. It was then that Wilbur Squillbur poured a bottle of concoction in his engine.

"RB I done like you, I modified some Horloff fuel through a reference stilling process."

The front of Wilbur Squillbur's boat went flying upward out of the water and into the air and almost capsized, front to back, as it lunged forward. As it came splashing back down and powered forward his two new friends Duffy and Lamont fell out.

Wilbur Squillbur kept his eyes on the finish line and won the race.

Afterword:

The Voyage of the Cauldron Skipper

I was inspired to write this novel from stories my father told me. Specifically of how my Great Grandfather fell in the Flambeau River near Butternut Wisconsin and was rescued by his Irish Setter and later how my Great Grandfather operated a sawmill the town of Loyal of Central Wisconsin and earlier went on to found the city of Theresa Wisconsin. My Great Grandfather later settled in an area now called Theresa. He was of strong character and integrity and liked to wrestle with the Indians there. My Great Grandmother Bridget did not want to live alone in the area and she told John, her husband when he was going to Milwaukee in the spring to get some settlers from there. So he came to Milwaukee and German settlers were enticed to settle in the area. They named it Theresa a German name for Therese.

The theme of going over the falls and the voyage home is a metaphor that I created for soul loss and recovery. A theme not just inspired by my Grandmother whom we visited when I was boy in Northern Wisconsin.

Thomas Paul Murphy

Thomas Paul Murphy

ABOUT THE AUTHOR

Born November 2nd 1966 in Wisconsin, I grew up in Whitefish Bay a suburb of Milwaukee. I graduated from the University of Wisconsin Milwaukee in 1991 with a Bachelor's Degree in Business Administration with a double major in Accounting and Finance. After a brief career in Equity Research and Accounting I have gone on to pursue creative interests and found a love for creative writing. I like sharing an understanding of humanity that is often missing in our popular culture and the creative focus of my writing is on psychology and our environment.

Thomas Paul Murphy